BEAGLES LOVE STEAK SECRETS

A SMALL TOWN CULINARY COZY MYSTERY

BEAGLE DINER MYSTERIES

C. A. PHIPPS

For my daughters who fill me with admiration at the women they have become.
You are amazing. xx

BEAGLES LOVE STEAK SECRETS

Out of the frying pan and into the fire!

Back in her hometown, everything is going great for ex-celebrity chef Lyra St Claire and her beagle, Cinnamon.

Until the sudden death of a friend.

As sad as the town is, another dark cloud hangs over the residents of Fairview. This was no accident!

The police have their suspicions, but if Lyra can't find out whodunnit soon, the diner might fail and someone could get away with murder.

Beagle Diner Cozy Mysteries are light and entertaining, with a bunch of clues, delicious baking and one clever beagle who can't say no.

Beagle Diner Cozy Mysteries

Beagles Love Cupcake Crimes
Beagles Love Steak Secrets
Beagles Love Muffin But Murder
Beagles Love Layer Cake Lies

Join my newsletter and pick up a your free bonus epilogue.

PROLOGUE

When celebrity chef Lyra St. Claire decided to make small-town Fairview her home, it came as a surprise to many, including herself.

Hosting a popular TV show, making appearances around the country judging competitions, and having owned one of the top restaurants in LA, she'd made the chalk-and-cheese leap in a ridiculously short space of time.

From the minute she returned to her birthplace, it took less than an hour to decide that she belonged here, and barely more than that to get the paperwork signed to purchase the run-down diner. The strangest thing of all was that unable to find the perfect house for herself and her mom in Portland, she had come to Fairview on a whim of nostalgia.

None of these events were easy to explain, and that explanation was going down like a lead balloon. The park seemed like the perfect place to discuss her rash decision and meant that Cinnamon her beagle could happily run around outside picking up new scents and bounding around their legs. Her antics usually amused everyone, but not today.

Kaden Hunter's mouth turned down from her first sentence and remained that way. "I can't pretend to be happy about it when I don't understand why you would rush into something like this."

He had every reason to feel this way. Having to sell her LA restaurant when most of her funds were stolen, the decision to settle in Portland where she'd trained and where Kaden's restaurant was seemed the most logical one. They could not only maintain their friendship, which had recently been reborn, but she could get away from far too many bad memories and the big-city rat race.

"I'm sorry. It is so far removed from anything we discussed, it's no wonder you feel disappointed. To be honest, I can't get my head around the speed with which it all happened. All I know is that I don't regret it. So far."

"But why did you jump into this so soon?" He raised an eyebrow. "Were you worried I'd try to talk you out of it?"

"Judging by your reaction, I guess you would have tried, but that didn't occur to me. The truth is, there wasn't time to call or wait until I saw you. A conglomerate was buying up everything, and they had a meeting set up with the owner that afternoon with an offer going on the table. It was, literally, now or never. I offered a fair price for the diner and the owner accepted." She snapped her fingers. "Just like that it was a done deal."

He shook his head, clearly confused. "How did buying a diner of all things come up when you were looking at houses?"

"I need a business and a house. If it was one or the other, I could manage financially, but there is nothing in Portland I can afford that would give me both. Especially now that Mom's coming to live with me."

"Surely selling her apartment would free up more funds?"

"Sure, but I don't know how long that will take and paying for hotel rooms for four people is crippling."

He grimaced. "I wish you'd said something. Despite the insurance payout for the fire, I don't have much in reserve, but I would gladly have helped. And you could have stayed with me and saved on rent."

She smiled gently. His restaurant had been the target of arson, meaning Kaden had also gone through his share of lean times. "That's so sweet of you, but I don't think you'd fit all of us in your apartment."

"I hadn't thought about all of you moving in." He snorted. "Can't Maggie and Dan get their own places?"

"They will when we settle somewhere, but I couldn't ask them to pay rent until I'm able to give them a decent wage. I need a job—and soon."

"What about the show and your guest appearances? They must pay well."

"*A Lesson with Lyra* was put on extended hiatus because of the court cases. Since I haven't heard when they might resume, I can't count on that income stream. As for the appearances, they dried up when I fired my agent. I guess he had more sway than I gave him credit for."

Kaden grimaced once more. "At least he's out of our lives."

Thankful that she would never have to deal with Simon Reeves ever again, Lyra still felt guilty that Kaden got caught up in the mess that her life had been a short time ago. Repaying him by moving away again had to hurt. "I'm truly sorry living nearby didn't work out."

"Well, I guess you've already signed the papers and I can't change that, but I will miss you," he said sadly.

"I'll miss you too, but Fairview isn't that far. We can visit far more easily than if I'd stayed in LA."

"I know; it's just I was looking forward to seeing you all the time."

Lyra laughed. "While it's a lovely idea, we both know that wouldn't have happened like we planned. We both work too hard, and your restaurant is only just getting back to where it was after the fire. You've been putting in long hours, and I will be too, no matter where I settle."

"I suppose that's true. I'd just hate for us to drift apart again."

He was referring to when she'd been plucked from obscurity at cooking school and had moved to LA. Her ex-agent found every way imaginable to keep them apart, and sadly he'd succeeded. It took Kaden a long time to forgive Lyra for giving up on their friendship, and she'd only recently forgiven herself. "I couldn't bear that either. Now that there's no outside interference, we can make this work."

"We *will* make it work," he stated, then took a deep breath. "Okay, tell me about this diner, and what about the house?"

Lyra screwed up her face. "The diner is truly awful. I'm not exaggerating. It's disgustingly filthy and outdated. The house is derelict and needs everything done to it as well. The owners just walked away due to family issues and haven't been back for years. A friend of my mom got in contact with them, and they jumped at the chance to off-load it."

Kaden crouched to take the stick from Cinnamon and give her a long awaited scratch before he looked up at Lyra. "I hate to break it to you, but neither sound appealing. Getting them up to scratch will be a lot of hard work and money."

She laughed. "You're not wrong. Although, I did get the house cheap, and luckily Dan is great with his hands, so he'll do most of the renovations, concentrating on the diner first, then move on to the house when time permits. Meanwhile, Maggie and I will do the cleaning especially at the house to make it livable and help Dan where we can. As you can tell, on the ride back here we made a few plans."

"You've always been good at seeing the bigger picture," he acknowledged while lines creased his forehead. "Are you sure you're up for this?"

She shrugged. "Maybe it's just a stepping-stone, but I'm looking forward to working in a different way. You know I didn't enjoy being in the limelight and hated having every aspect of my life put under a microscope. This venture excites me in a way I can't explain."

"I can see that." Kaden sighed. "You finally look like the happy-go-lucky girl I trained with. LA took a toll on you, didn't it?"

"It was rough," she admitted. "But not all bad. I had money to help other aspiring chefs, and my charity work with rescue animals kept me sane. Then there was La Joliesse, the restaurant of my heart—" Her voice hitched. "Certainly, there were things I couldn't have achieved without the fame."

He nodded. "So, you can afford to do this without a loan?"

They didn't have secrets anymore, so it would be silly to take offense. "I'll be fine. At least the new apartment I bought before everything went wrong sold quickly, and that money will come through soon. Plus, I have the advance for the new cookbook I'm writing and the royalties from the others are still trickling in. Sorry if I gave the impression that I was broke." She grinned. "I guess there was some panic involved, and maybe I gave up the restaurant too quickly, but I don't regret getting out of that lifestyle."

"Well, I do want you to be happy. You deserve it after dealing with murder and saying goodbye to La Joliesse. If you need a bit to tide you over, let me know."

She should have known he'd offer, yet she was still touched. "Thanks. Your support means so much. I'll be busy getting both places usable, plus I have that new cookbook out in a couple of months which needs some love, but I hope you'll come take a look around when the place looks a little better."

Kaden snorted. "You couldn't keep me away. When are you moving there?"

"As soon as I can to save on rent. Once the diner is up and running, I can concentrate on the house, but first I'll need to find staff. Mom's friend assures me he can recommend a couple of people." She chuckled. "I saved the best news for last."

He raised an eyebrow. "I can't wait to hear this."

She laughed at his sarcasm but was extra excited about this part and couldn't hide it. "The house is actually the same farmhouse that I grew up in, and I worked in the diner when I was a teenager. I really am going home."

Finally, he laughed. "Just seeing you light up that way puts it into perspective. I couldn't picture you in a diner after seeing you in La Joliesse. She seemed to be everything you wanted, a true beauty, and this will be… well, not the same," he finished lamely.

"You're right, it can't ever be the same. Nothing I do after owning my dream restaurant would be, but different doesn't have to be bad. Maybe it won't work out, but I'm looking forward to trying."

"Then I wish you all the best with your new adventure. You better get something for me to sleep on, because I'm coming down to visit as often as I can. I'll bring a sleeping bag if necessary."

He made it sound like a threat, but Lyra knew better and threw her arms around him. "You'll always be welcome, anytime."

"Likewise, and you better reciprocate."

"Oh, I will," she said into his shoulder. "A little bit of fancy from time to time will be welcome."

"In that case, I'm going to make you the best meal ever, so you never forget me again."

"As if I could." As he held her tight, Lyra could have added that the murders of innocent people, not to mention the anxiety and stress over the long-running mystery tainting her life for so long, were the things she needed to forget. Or at least get over. All she knew for sure was that this felt like the best way to do that.

Arm in arm they walked back to his restaurant for the promised meal. Cinnamon ran ahead, coming back constantly to check on them, as they discussed ideas for the diner menu. With Kaden on board with her scheme, Lyra's heart was lighter. Now all she had to do, apart from wait for all the legalities to be finalized, was tell Mom.

1

The Beagle Diner was full of the lunchtime crowd. It had been this way ever since Lyra hung the open sign on her door a few months ago. Though the small town of Fairview was still curious about the ex-celebrity chef, the first few weeks were more about the press than the food, and she was relieved when that died down.

Many of the locals found the opening exciting and came out in their Sunday best, hoping to be seen on the news or featured in a paper somewhere. Naturally, there were one or two who took umbrage at the town being turned upside down, but no one could argue with the influx of business the area had seen.

Maggie Parker sat outside the back of the diner at a table in the corner of the pet-friendly covered veranda. She was working on Lyra's latest cookbook and keeping an eye on the customers out there. Cinnamon, sat at Maggie's feet, and whenever anyone came by, she introduced herself. Seated in this prime position in the center of town since day one, the beagle was already well-known.

Lyra dropped off an order and hurried back to the counter inside.

"Are these fresh?"

Lyra blinked in surprise. Arabelle Filmore was a cranky woman in her sixties, who'd exhausted her ageist get-out-of-jail-free card by saying what she thought whenever she felt like it.

"The cupcakes are just out of the oven, Ms. Filmore."

Arabelle sniffed. "If that were true, the frosting would be melting."

"Did you want one?" Lyra held a set of tongs in her hand, thinking what she'd like to do with them had nothing to do with food, and smiled.

"Don't rush me. I'm still thinking about it."

"Take as long as you need." Lyra put the tongs down. The problem with waiting for Arabelle was that she refused to move out of the way or take a seat, and the line grew.

"I'll get my usual, please," Robert McKenna called over the top of the tiny woman's head.

"You wait your turn, Robert McKenna!" Arabelle scolded.

He shrugged. "If we did that every time you dithered around in here, we'd starve."

Arabelle looked him up and down and sniffed. "I can't see that happening."

Also in his sixties, Rob was as fit as a man half his age. Grinning, he patted his slightly rounded stomach. "It's all bought and paid for, Belle. Thanks for noticing, though."

Arabelle sucked in a large breath. "Don't you dare call me that!"

Rob laughed. "You were Belle as a kid and, as far as I'm concerned, still Belle now."

Feathers well and truly ruffled, Arabelle's mouth opened and closed several times. Arabelle being lost for words was a sight Lyra hadn't seen before. She took that moment to send

Rob's order through to the kitchen, then waited, along with every customer in earshot, for Arabelle to focus.

"All that fat will kill you," Arabelle finally managed through clenched teeth.

Rob took a seat and blew her a cheeky kiss. "You're such a caring woman, can't think why you haven't been snapped up long ago."

"That man has no respect," Arabelle grumbled. "I'll have my usual."

Lyra had to bite her lip yet wasn't surprised by the choice. No matter what caught her eye, Arabelle always had tea and a berry friand.

From where he sat, Rob rolled his eyes, and Lyra had to look away as she took the money. The two of them were as funny as a play and still amusing even though it ran every day.

The waitress hurriedly cleaned the table that Arabelle preferred, which had fortunately become vacant. Twenty-year-old Poppy received no thanks and moved on to take orders from the diners who waited with a good deal more patience and politeness. Having a sweet but no-nonsense disposition, unless her mom Vanessa was about, Poppy was perfect for the job of waitress and barista. It meant that Lyra was comfortable leaving her to deal with the diners so she could get back to the kitchen and ensure orders weren't backing up.

This was the beauty of a small business. She could cook or chat with her customers or spend time on a new recipe when things were quiet. After a horrendous few months dealing with two different types of crimes, she concluded that her previous life as a celebrity chef and show host was overrated. She did miss her famous LA restaurant, La Joliesse, but she could cook anywhere and that's what meant the most to her—not fame, which went hand in hand with being hounded by fans and paparazzi. Just the thought made her shudder.

Even with her daily dose of Arabelle, which Lyra tried not to inflict on her staff, she didn't regret her decision to move from LA to Fairview instead of staying in Portland, her original choice, and opening a more upmarket restaurant rather than a diner.

This pretty town lay halfway between there and Destiny to the south and meant a huge change of life for not only herself but some of her staff. Most remained at La Joliesse after the sale, while a couple opted to join her in this adventure. Of course, Fairview was Lyra's childhood home, so she did have an advantage over the others.

The main street had a cross intersection in the middle and a few more roads bisecting each arm of it. Some buildings were two-story with apartments above the businesses, but most were single-storied like the diner. At the back was the veranda Lyra added to make the covered dining area. Behind this was a gravel parking lot and path, then a hedge and, slightly visible beyond, was an old farmhouse. This was Lyra's home, and it couldn't be more convenient.

The day she'd driven here on a whim with her assistant, Maggie, and her driver, Dan, they found a run-down diner and a derelict farmhouse. A conglomerate working with the town committee was buying up the businesses, and Rob McKenna persuaded Lyra to purchase the diner, thereby saving it and possibly the town. Dramatics aside, the local lawyer made it happen that day, and once the bill of sale came through, the rest was history.

The farmhouse took a bit longer to buy since the owners had to be tracked down, but within a month it was hers. Still a work in progress, the house had to wait because the diner needed a top-to-toe refit, which had to come first.

Engrossed in her late afternoon prep work and rolling

out the pastry for her chicken pies, Lyra marveled as she often did at the change in the diner from front to back, now that it was finished.

A hand touched her shoulder. "You're miles away."

Lyra dropped the rolling pin on her foot and yelped. Cinnamon barked from the doorway, and Maggie took a step back.

"Sorry, I didn't mean to startle you."

"I'm okay," she said to both and swept her long red hair back over her shoulder. "I was thinking about all the changes and how I still can't believe how far we've come in such a short time."

Maggie grinned. "Shall I pinch you?"

"No need for more violence. Besides, I know by my rough hands that I'm working harder than I ever have."

"You don't seem upset by that," Maggie mused. "No regrets?"

"Not yet. How about you?"

Maggie grinned again. "How you talked me into this I'll never know, but I am glad about it."

Lyra smirked. "I don't remember twisting your arm."

"I admit it's way less stressful than making sure your itinerary didn't blow out and that you had everything you needed for each trip. Now I get to work on the book and the house, which are both things I love."

"I'm glad too." Lyra cut the pastry to line the two dozen pans set out on the counter. "You're an amazing designer, and doing this without you would have been a nightmare."

"I doubt that," Maggie argued, while looking pleased. "You love a challenge."

"I guess that must be true, since I've had plenty of them."

Maggie snorted. "There were definitely several that you could have done without, but look how much you've achieved in a few months."

Lyra glanced around her and nodded. "I guess I have to accept that my previous life paid for all this and be grateful."

All she'd wanted was to live in peace doing what she loved, and now that's exactly what she had. Of course, it couldn't be so successful without her staff. In the doorway, Poppy retied her hair, then she washed her hands. The girl was a quick learner, adored by Cinnamon, and keen to be a chef. Likewise, the lanky and earnest dishwasher, Earl, who was simply happy to have a job what with his learning difficulty, often cleared tables if they got swamped. Leroy, her cook, was the major find, thanks to Rob. Hiring him meant he could handle the grill, which left her to concentrate on the baking.

As if fate decided there was too much happiness going on, the back door opened, and Dan burst in.

"There's been a flood in the house. I need a bigger mop!" He pulled it from the large bucket in the utility room and ran back outside.

Maggie hurried out behind him.

Lyra ripped off her apron. "Will you be okay, Leroy?"

"Get going! I'll be fine, and the others will help."

Lyra didn't doubt her chef. Leroy was a blessing. He took it in his stride when she ducked in and out of the diner to take care of house queries and to work on her book. Finding him made running a diner instead of a restaurant more palatable than she had ever imagined.

After throwing a damp cloth over the pastry, she ran after Dan and Maggie.

2

Cinnamon waited at the door with wet paws. Lyra followed her prints and two other drier sets of human shoe prints to the main bathroom, which was full of steam. Dan moved back, as did Maggie who pointed at the new mirror.

Lyra frowned, then sloshed through an inch of water which had been prevented from seeping into the hallway by a mountain of towels, to where words were scrawled diagonally across the glass in condensation. Now that the hot water was turned off and the window opened, the words were fading and a couple of letters had disappeared, but it was still readable.

You don't belong here!

A shiver ran up Lyra's back. "What the heck is this about?"

"I've got no idea." Dan pointed to a sodden towel at his feet. "Whoever turned the tap on placed a towel along the door so that the water would back up. It's not too bad considering I don't know how long the tap was running, but we'll have to wait for the floor to dry out completely before the tiles go down. That will set us back a few days."

His practicality almost made her smile. Solving another mystery so soon after the last shambles was not on Lyra's plan, and it made her angry. "I don't care so much about that. The note and towel mean this was done deliberately, and I want to know why this person wants me gone. Plus, how did someone get in here without you or Cinnamon noticing?"

Dan dipped his head. "Cinnamon looked bored over by the diner, and I hadn't had my lunch, so I took her and my sandwich down by the stream. I didn't think to lock up."

He looked so miserable that Lyra forced herself to take a deep breath. "This is not your fault. We've all become lax because this isn't LA or Portland and no one seems to take security too seriously around here."

"But you're not just anyone," Maggie pointed out. "You have fans who take liberties. They won't all disappear because you're no longer hosting a show. There is cable you know, and reruns worldwide."

"You don't seriously think a fan has followed me here?" The shiver from before reached her voice.

"Anything is possible, but that's only one scenario." Maggie attempted to reassure her. "There was a lot of drama around you buying the diner because the conglomerate wanted the whole main street knocked down and remodeled. Plus, there were those who were worried that you would bring big-city ways to town. Or maybe it's someone who wanted the diner for something else."

Lyra clenched her hands. "No matter the reason, I won't be run out of town. We need to find this troublemaker before they do something else."

"I'd like to point out that it could be a one-off," Dan suggested hopefully.

"Perhaps." Lyra liked his optimism, but she couldn't let

things get out of hand the way they had in Portland and LA when she hadn't followed up hard enough after several crimes. "Meanwhile, let's make sure the house and diner are locked up if no one's there. I'll head over to the police station and tell them what happened in case they want to see the mirror or check for fingerprints around the house."

Cinnamon decided to tag along, but they were hardly down the steps when the beagle stopped. Nose twitching, she turned away from Lyra and disappeared around the side of the house. Lyra hesitated; she still had pies to fill after visiting the police, but her dog was clearly on a mission. Cinnamon sniffed around underneath the bathroom, then looked up and barked.

"What is it, girl?"

The beagle sat and lifted her right paw, still looking up. There was a slight slope leading down to the stream, and a small tree sat close to the window. From one of the branches hung a hat. Lyra stretched up on her tippy toes and yanked it free.

Fairview Forever was emblazoned on the rim. "I've seen these around, Cin. Do you think the person who broke in and left the taps on dropped this?"

The beagle wagged her tail and looked up again as Dan poked his head out the open window.

"I thought I heard you talking." He smirked.

"Look what Cinnamon found on that shrub." Lyra waved the hat at him. "Did you leave the bathroom window open when you were out?"

He blinked. "Now that you mention it, I thought I had, but it was closed when I got back."

"Hmmm. That implies that the person either went in or came out the window," Lyra mused. "Maybe both. Perhaps while they were trying to close the window, they lost the hat."

Maggie joined Dan at the window and leaned on the sash. "That makes sense because there were no wet footprints inside the house other than ours. They had to have left this way unless they didn't wait for the sink to overflow."

"The hot water had to run a while to fog the mirror, and the window would need to be closed." Lyra paced around the tree. "Can you see there are a couple of broken branches at the top? They have to be strong enough to hold their weight, so it can't be a small person."

"Although, those branches aren't terribly thick," Maggie noted.

"You reached the hat," Dan pointed out. "Which means the person must be shorter than you."

"True, but maybe they heard you arrive, were in a hurry to get away, and simply didn't have time to collect the hat."

Rob McKenna poked his head around the corner. "Seems like a funny place to have a party."

"No party; it's more of a brainstorm," Lyra explained. "Somebody broke into the house and turned a tap on. The bathroom was flooded, but Dan caught it in time before it spread through the rest of the house."

"Well done, lad. That could have been nasty after all your hard work. Any ideas on the culprit?"

"None, but they left this hat hanging on a shrub." Lyra held it out to him.

"It looks pretty worn, but I'm sorry to say that most residents have one of them, including me." Rob shrugged. "Seems to me that it could have been left by anyone at any time."

"Really?" Lyra twisted the hat in her hands. "That's a shame. I thought it was a great clue."

"Sorry to burst your bubble. The town committee got a bunch of them made up when we had a fishing competition a while ago. It was back when we were being proactive about getting tourists and some new residents."

"You mean that not only people from Fairview might have one of these caps?"

"Unfortunately, that's likely true."

"Darn it." Lyra sighed. "I thought we might be onto something."

"Well, if anyone says they lost their cap, I'll let you know," Rob said, deadpan.

He loved to tease, and this wasn't such a big deal, but what if it heralded the beginning of something worse? While she wasn't naturally pessimistic, recent history had slightly scarred her optimism about such things. "I guess the likelihood of that happening is remote. Since it's not life-or-death, we haven't rung the police, but I'm going to the station to report this."

"I'll come with you," he offered. "Sheriff Walker can be hard to talk to."

Lyra didn't doubt that. The times he came in for coffee or a bite he had stared far too much for her liking. He was good-looking with short brown hair which made his cool gray eyes even more startling. And piercing. She got the impression he didn't know what to make of her and she felt the same about him.

"In that case, I'll be glad of the company." She looked up to find Dan and Maggie gazing at each other. "Could you two clean up the water, but leave the mirror and keep Cinnamon here?"

It could have been the sun warming their faces, but both were pink-cheeked.

"Leave it to us," Dan called, then moved back into the room.

The station wasn't far. They crossed the street at the end of Lyra's drive, went up the road, and passed a couple of houses. When they got to the corner, they crossed again. The station was five doors down, and Rob explained that it was usually manned by three police officers. Also, the sheriff had towns to the east and west that he oversaw, so he wasn't always there.

The few times she'd seen him in the street, or when he'd stopped by for coffee, he'd given her a penetrating look that was both embarrassing and annoying. Naturally he would have heard rumors about her troubled past and quite possibly investigated them. Which should have exonerated her from anything that he could dig up. Whatever his reason for being less than friendly, she didn't like it one bit.

"I hope this isn't our designated walk for today. Even if you have provided a little more drama than usual," Rob teased.

"You can't get out of it that easily. Besides, Cinnamon won't be happy that we've left her behind."

He nodded. "She does like her freedom."

Rob opened the door for Lyra, and inside they found the desk clerk reading a romance novel. Her badge read Officer Moore, and when she noticed them, she quickly stuffed the book under the counter.

"Ms. St. Claire, what can I do for you?" she gushed.

Lyra had seen this kind of reaction so many times it hardly affected her, and she quickly explained the situation. When she finished, the clerk blinked several times before responding.

"Goodness, that's a tricky one. With almost everyone owning a hat like that, I don't know how we can say who did this."

Lyra breathed deeply. "Officer Moore, I appreciate that right now we can't pin it on anyone, and the writing on the mirror will be gone," Belatedly, it occurred to her that she should have taken a photo, "but is there a chance that someone could come take a look at the crime scene?"

The officer shot a longing glance at where she'd stowed the book. "I guess it couldn't hurt. Let me speak to the sheriff."

Lyra sighed as the woman disappeared out the back and took a seat on a hard wooden bench. "We might be here a while."

"It could be worse." Rob dropped the words enigmatically and sat beside her.

They waited for ten minutes, scanning all the brochures on display, until the sheriff appeared. Tall and roughly Dan's build, his hair was pressed down on top as if he'd recently worn a hat. He ran those cool gray eyes over Lyra, then grimaced at Rob.

"Officer Moore told me about your problem, Ms. St. Claire. It seems a little far-fetched that someone would break in to cause a flood. Are you sure that your handyman didn't leave the tap on?"

His dismissive attitude rankled, and it was an effort to be polite. "Thank you for seeing us. I understand that it's not much to go on, but if Dan had done that, he would have told me so. And why would he leave a note on the mirror telling me I didn't belong here when he lives in my house? Also, I know he doesn't have a cap like this." Lyra handed it to him.

The sheriff turned it over a couple of times in an unconcerned manner. "While it's commendable that you trust your handyman, it just doesn't seem like something that would happen around here. Maybe Dan would prefer to get back to the big city sooner than you thought. Now that the major building has been completed, an ex-army man probably has a few more abilities other than doing odd jobs. As for the cap, I'm sure Rob told you they're a dime a dozen and could have been left there by anyone before you showed up— or after."

Lyra stiffened at the mention of Dan wanting more than working for her. It sounded as though the sheriff had been doing some checks on the town's newest inhabitants and made a few judgements. "I can assure you that Dan is free to leave whenever he chooses and has no need to make up ridiculous scenarios to do so. Finding out why that cap was stuck in a tree outside my bathroom would be a better question?"

He shrugged. "It gets windy around town. I dare say it blew there."

"Since I've been in Fairview, it hasn't been windy at all."

Sheriff Walker narrowed his eyes as if she'd called him a liar. "Lucky for you. Now, if you're done, I need to get back to solving real crimes for our residents."

Irritated by his dismissal, Lyra noted he kept the cap.

"Thanks for dropping by. I do love your food, and your show was amazing," Officer Moore gushed. "It's such a shame that you lost it."

Lyra simply nodded as they left. People couldn't appreciate that she was happy to give up her fame for a diner in Fairview. "How about that? He wasn't the slightest bit interested," she told Rob when they got outside the door.

"I confess that I was curious if you'd have more sway with Walker than me. Since he was giving me the side-eye, I decided to keep my mouth shut, but it seems he treats most people with the same disdain."

"I guess a flood isn't high on a priority list. We were lucky that Dan found it when he did."

"Don't you fret. As much as it doesn't seem like it, the sheriff doesn't like drama in his towns, so he won't sit by and do nothing, and I'll keep an eye on the house."

The sheriff's style of working was certainly interesting, but she wasn't satisfied with the outcome. "Even if we all took turns, it's not possible to watch it all day. We have businesses to run, and Dan and Maggie are busy too."

"I take on less work these days, so I have time to wander by. I'll make it known around town that there was a break-in. If someone's worried about getting caught, they won't like that, and the rest of us will be more vigilant."

"Thanks for the help, but last thing I want is for you to put yourself in danger."

"A person who turns on a tap isn't likely bent on physically hurting another." Rob scratched the top of his head. "In my opinion, your tap-turner is a coward."

"I hope you're right. Please be careful, and call Dan if you see anything. Now, I better get my pies done, the pastry will be ruined and I'll have to start over."

About to part company at the corner, Rob raised an eyebrow. "We can't have that. Perhaps I better check one to make sure they're okay before you try to sell any."

Lyra groaned. "Another tester—just what I need. Come by in an hour, and they'll be ready."

"No need to twist my arm." He waved and swaggered toward his garage, several doors down the street from their houses.

One of the unforeseen pleasures of coming home to Fairview was her next-door neighbor always made her laugh.

3

Lyra's pies had sold out when Rob turned up at dinner time. In fact, Leroy had finished them off for her while she was out since the dough would likely have been unusable by the time she got back. Poppy had gone home, and Lyra and Maggie were eating omelets at one of the tables in the diner.

"Sorry I couldn't make it any earlier and we missed our walk." Rob grimaced. "Wish I hadn't bothered, but a customer needed an urgent job."

They'd walked together every day since the week she moved into town and Lyra enjoyed hearing him talk about life here and especially stories that featured her dad. She always came back to work with a smile.

"Lucky I kept my promise. I kept one back just for you. I'll get it warmed up."

"You're a gem, Lyra. Where's Dan got to, Maggie?"

"He's house watching. Don't worry about him missing out on dinner, he's got enough food over there to feed an army."

"I suspect a man his size needs plenty to keep up his strength, what with all that hard work." Rob winked. "Plus,

27

he has to fight off the ladies in town, and not all of them are single."

Lyra caught the conversation and wink, as had the customers who had their eyes on Maggie.

"Who, Dan?" Her assistant laughed loudly. "He's married with a bunch of kids and a feisty wife. He has to work hard so he can send them all his money."

Lyra almost dropped the plate and pie. She'd never heard Maggie tell a lie, and it was a shock. As far as she knew, Dan didn't even have a girlfriend. The penny dropped as soon as she saw Maggie's face.

Red-cheeked, Maggie could hardly meet her gaze, so Lyra carried on as if nothing were amiss. If Maggie was harboring feelings for Dan, and she'd bet a batch of chocolate muffins on it being reciprocated, who was she to get in their way? She'd also bet a tray of pies that no other woman hereabouts would chase him when these customers spread the word about Dan's family.

It was naughty, but hilarious, and Lyra wondered what Dan would say when it got back to him. As it surely would.

Rob turned his amused glance from Maggie and cut into his pie. He inhaled loudly. "So, I was telling you about this customer who needed his car fixed ASAP. Never seen him in my life, but he's asking all these questions about Fairview." He took a large mouthful and chewed thoughtfully before he swallowed. "He wore these big sunglasses which hid most of his face. His jacket looked two sizes too big, and the collar hugged his cheeks. Mighty odd if you ask me, when it's hardly cold out. He had the biggest beard I've ever seen. Looked like he'd plastered a squirrel on his face."

She laughed at the vision, but after this morning's drama, this seemed an odd coincidence to Lyra. "Was he passing through?"

"He was hardly full of information he wanted to share,

but I did get that much out of him. Said he was only staying until the car was fixed. Oddly, he spent the whole time walking around the garage and watching me. Of course, folks hereabouts do that all the time, but someone you don't know watching you is disconcerting."

"I imagine it would be. Then again, I've been watched for years. Some people have no boundaries and assume others don't mind."

"You mean to tell me that I'm famous?" Rob snorted.

Lyra grinned. "In Fairview, for sure."

He winked. "Anyway, I was coming here and got stopped by Martha Curran. You know, one of your mom's friends?"

"Yes, she's been into the diner a few times since I opened to chat about Mom."

"Well, Martha knows everyone, and she happened to mention that this guy looked around every shop in town and never bought a darn thing. Doesn't sound like a tourist, right?"

"He never came in here that I know about. Maybe he didn't need anything except to get his car fixed."

"That's just it. When he's done wandering Fairview, he comes to me and complains about his car not working right. Why wouldn't he come see me first?"

Lyra nodded. "I see your point, but if he's never been here before, he might not have known where your business was or if there are others to choose from. Perhaps he was asking around."

Rob slapped his thigh. "Shoot. That does make sense. Guess I have too much time on my hands after all."

Lyra laughed. "Weren't you the one who said we don't need more drama in Fairview?"

"That's for sure." Maggie pointedly touched the wooden table.

Rob rolled his eyebrows. "I believe it was the sheriff who

made that statement, missy. I forgot to say that the man barely thanked me for staying open to fix his car, but he didn't quibble over the price."

"That's because you don't charge enough for your services," Lyra told him.

He grinned. "Just for that, I might buy a slice of pie for dessert."

"No need. Poppy took some to Dan earlier. Enough for both of you."

"Goodness, I have fallen on my feet by taking your friend in."

"He says the same about you."

Rob wiped his face, suddenly solemn. "I could never say I missed company, except for my wife's, but Dan and I have a lot in common. I hope he likes staying as much as I enjoy having him there."

Lyra nodded. "He does and is very grateful to be at your place rather than at a hotel or in a room that needs work from top to toe like he had at my house."

"Good to know, but it hardly seems fair when that's what he ended up with by moving into my spare room. I'm embarrassed to say I haven't done much with the place for so long, which never bothered me until Dan came to stay. That boy's got some talent. He's done a lot of things already, including fixing up two doors that wouldn't shut properly and the leaky guttering. Next he plans to paint inside." Rob sighed. "The place hasn't seen so much love in decades."

"I guess between my place and yours, Dan's got plenty of work to keep him busy, and he did a wonderful job on the diner."

Rob looked around them. "He did indeed. I remember coming here with your parents when the place wasn't half as fancy as this. You all tucked up in the pram, or sitting on a chair when you got bigger, and taking everything in. Why, I even recall you developed a talent for deciding what should stay on the menu or go."

There was something wonderful about hearing someone talk about your past this way, and Lyra hung on his every word. "As a child I could dictate that?"

"Sure. You wouldn't even taste something if you didn't like the look of it. The owner back then got so he trusted your opinion. That's why your food is so popular—it looks as good as it tastes every single time."

Lyra grinned. "That's the nicest thing I've heard in a long while."

"Now, that is a crying shame. You have more talent in your little finger than anyone I know and deserve compliments every day."

"I agree. Some people wouldn't know great food if it came wrapped in gold," Maggie complained. "Lyra's new cookbook should take care of that."

"I hope not." Lyra grimaced. "At least around here. I do want it to sell heaps of copies because I have a lot of renovations still to do, but I don't want people coming to town to gawk at me. There was enough of that in the first few months after I opened. Besides, Leroy does most of the cooking."

"Under your watchful eye." Maggie shot a look over to Leroy. "He's very good, but this is your diner, and it's your name behind it. People love that a famous chef resides in Fairview, and they can't figure out why, because to them you're still a celebrity and they picture you in a fancier setting."

"Tourists having a reason to come to Fairview will benefit everyone, not just the diner." Leroy nodded sagely. "It's wonderful that you help so many local businesses just by being here."

Lyra felt a familiar pressure. When she had an agent and a

slew of people to support, it felt as though she could never say no to more work. This was a major part of her decision to leave that life behind her and search for a more peaceful existence where she was just Lyra, owner of the diner. Was it terribly selfish to not want more for Fairview, simply because it suited her to live a little off the grid?

Maybe, but how could she stop the fascination with her cooking, or her fall from fame, if she kept promoting herself with cookbooks? It's not like she was hard to find when the books announced to the world all over again exactly where she was.

Lyra shivered. What was the alternative?

4

_____

The next day Lyra had an opportunity to speak to Sheriff Walker. It would be fair to say she didn't relish it. He came in for coffee, but while she poured a cup, Lyra noticed he had his eyes on the cottage pies.

"They're fresh this morning," she assured him. "Or would you like a menu?"

He motioned at the sign on the heated display case. "What's in a cottage pie?"

This was the first pleasant conversation they'd had and Lyra responded as she usually would with any other customer. "It's a savory meat dish, topped with mashed potato and cheese. They're great for lunch, or you could add vegetables and eat it for dinner."

He checked his watch. "I guess it is nearly lunchtime."

"Do you want to eat in here or out on the veranda? It is lovely outside today." She headed down the short hall, and thankfully he followed.

"Is this okay?" Placing the cup down on a table furthest from the door, she stood back so he could take a seat. "It's quiet and sheltered in this corner. I'll get you that pie."

If he noticed her manipulation, the sheriff didn't say, and she hurried back inside.

"Was that the sheriff?" Poppy asked.

"Yes. He's having lunch."

"Goodness. I didn't think he liked you."

"Poppy!" Leroy scolded. "That's not very nice."

"It's only what I heard."

"We've had a little disagreement, but that happens, and it's nothing major."

Poppy pouted a little. "Except he always seems to be angry with someone."

"He does have an important and serious job to do, so we shouldn't judge him too harshly." *Where had that come from?* Even Maggie looked surprised at Lyra sticking up for the sheriff. Pretending not to notice, she went ahead with heating the pie.

"Here you are." She unloaded the tray and placed the pie, cutlery, napkin, and condiments in front of the sheriff.

"Thank you." Dosing his meal liberally with salt, he suddenly realized she wasn't leaving. "Was there something you wanted to say?"

Too much salt was bad for a person, sprung to her mind first. Lyra twisted her apron in both hands and took a deep breath. "I take it Rob hasn't mentioned a stranger in town?"

Deliberately, he wiped the cutlery with his napkin. "No, he didn't. I guess you're about to."

"Look, I know we didn't get off to a great start…"

He shifted uncomfortably in his seat. "Are you referring to your flood?"

"The break in," she corrected. "And the suspicious way you look at me"

His nostrils flared. "You're imagining things. Perhaps you could get whatever it is off your chest before my lunch goes cold."

This wasn't going to plan, and the apron got another wringing while she deliberated whether to challenge him some more, but this wasn't all about her. "Rob tells me he saw a stranger in town yesterday who hung around the garage while his car was fixed."

"He never mentioned anything to me, and it hardly sounds like a need for police intervention."

"But what if he was the person who broke into my house?"

He sighed heavily. "Here's what I think. If the tap wasn't left on by accident, and the hat was left in the tree by a child playing around, then we could assume that they got inside and decided to play a prank. Does that sound feasible?"

"Well, sure, but—"

"It makes as much sense as anything, and there were no footprints around your house to suggest otherwise. A man would have to at least flatten grass to more of an extent than what I saw."

"You went to the house?"

"No need to sound so shocked. I check out all leads, including the much talked about stranger in town who was never seen again. And before you ask, Rob didn't mention it, but plenty of others did. He was a tourist just passing through."

"Oh. I assumed that your dismissive attitude meant that you wouldn't bother."

Lines across his forehead deepened. "Your dim view of me is very obvious."

"Then I guess it matches yours of me."

They stared at each other for several moments until he broke eye contact and tapped the plate with his knife. "I can assure you that however we feel about each other, has no bearing on how I treat a case. When there is one. May I be allowed to finish my meal in peace, as promised?"

"Certainly." She marched into the kitchen more confused than earlier. Yet, he had been to the house to check and explained his theory, which appeased her somewhat. As did the whole stranger business. So why was she still annoyed with him? Because he thought her untrustworthy or intent on making up trouble where there was none? Her previous life had no doubt tainted his perception of her, but surely he could see she was doing her best to fit in and had never flaunted her fame.

She stood at her desk pondering this until she looked up to find the staff watching her closely—Maggie and Leroy with smirks. They were impossible!

5

Lyra had gotten into the habit of going to work early in the mornings, then leaving earlier at night. She couldn't work all the hours they were open as well as cook, so it suited her this way. She'd been there a couple of hours making bread and buns when Dan appeared at the diner door. The look on his face was almost a replica of the one two days ago. Except, he seemed far more anxious and upset.

He gulped and rubbed his face with both hands, and she noticed his eyes were slightly red. A chill ran down her spine. "Dan, are you okay?"

He gulped again. "I'm not hurt. But I thought you should be the first to know, aside from the police…"

She was confused by his hesitancy; she couldn't recall hearing any sirens. "Is it the house again? Is Maggie okay?"

Dan shook his head. "It's not that, and I haven't seen Maggie this morning. There's no easy way to say this. Rob's dead."

Lyra dropped onto a chair, tears blinding her. "Oh, no. How did it happen?"

"I'm not sure." Dan sat beside her and rubbed at his face

again. "He passed away last night sometime—so the paramedics said. I found him this morning in his garage at the house. He said he had a couple of things to finish, and I wasn't to wait up. I should have checked on him."

"Stop that. He wouldn't have wanted you to feel guilty."

"I can't help it. Usually, we have breakfast together and I'd made fresh coffee. When he didn't show I checked his room, but he never sleeps in, so I wasn't surprised that he wasn't there. The garage seemed the most logical place, and that's where I found him—behind some car parts he was cleaning up."

Lyra could picture Rob surrounded by the things he loved, and her eyes misted again. "This is so sad. He was such a sweetie. Did he fall and hurt himself?"

"I didn't see any evidence of that. The paramedics talked about a possible heart attack but wouldn't say for sure."

"Really? He was at the diner last night for his dinner, and he seemed his usual cheerful self. He certainly ate a hearty meal."

"The garage and his side projects kept him busy and fit," Dan agreed. "Since I got here, we spent a lot of time together. He helped me and I helped him. Never once did he complain or couldn't keep up. Although he did say he was tired a few times. Why didn't I make him slow down?" He rubbed his hands over his face. "It was hard to watch him being taken away like that."

Lyra stood and put her arms around him for a moment. She'd never seen Dan so emotional, and it spoke to how much he'd come to regard Rob. They all had. "You should have called us. It's never easy to see someone dead. Especially someone you care about. How about I make us fresh coffee? I know I could use some."

"I'd appreciate it." He sighed heavily. "I guess I was in shock and didn't know what to do apart from staying with him. Once the paramedics left, I mooched around thinking I should contact someone, but he never spoke about his family, and there are no pictures around his house except those of his late wife." Dan studied his hands. "I didn't think it right to go through his things, so I've left that to the police."

"That was the right thing to do. Someone around here will know his history. I feel bad that I never asked. Adults don't tend to confide in kids, and there never seemed to be an opportunity when I came back. When I think about it, Rob always steered the conversation, encouraging us to talk about ourselves." Lyra snapped her fingers. "We should ask Arabelle. They were arguing yesterday, and Rob said something a while ago about knowing her when they were kids."

"Good idea. Will she be in today?"

"She comes in every day." Lyra grimaced, then shook herself. "I suspect she's lonely."

"If she made an effort to be nice, that wouldn't be the case," Dan said testily.

Lyra nodded. "She can't seem to help herself. Especially around Rob. He was such a character and had her well pegged."

"Do you think I could move back into one of the unfinished rooms at your place until I can sort out a room at the hotel?"

"Of course, you can. I suppose it would be weird to stay there when Rob's gone."

"Exactly. If he does have family and they turn up, it would be awkward to have a lodger hanging about."

They drank their coffee in companionable silence until Leroy arrived.

"You two look glummer than Arabelle Filmore on a bad day."

Dan and Lyra stared at him.

"What did I say wrong?"

Dan explained how he'd found poor Rob that morning. The retelling wasn't easy for him.

Leroy was naturally blindsided. He coughed and blinked a few times. "I don't know what to say, except this is terrible news. Rob was a great guy."

"Did you know him well outside of the diner?" Lyra was suddenly appalled. She'd never asked Leroy what he liked to do when he wasn't at work, just as she'd made assumptions about Rob's day-to-day life. Rob must have had other friends, and he and Leroy got on well.

Leroy nodded sadly. "He wasn't a big drinker, but he'd come down to the bar on a Saturday night and we'd meet up after I closed the diner. We played a few games of darts and chatted, as you do. It wasn't set in stone but was pretty regular."

"Do you know if he had any family?"

"I believe he had a wife, but she died some years back. He never mentioned children. In fact, he didn't talk much about himself."

Lyra nodded. "I noticed that too. Did he have a lot of friends?"

"That's a tricky one." Leroy thought for a moment. "He was friendly with a lot of people. Fixing cars, he knew mostly everyone around town, but he didn't go to parties or things like that. If he wasn't in his garage down the road, he was in the one at home. Apart from Saturday nights."

Lyra sighed. "I guess we'll find out more as the day goes on. Or should we close for the day? I don't like the idea of carrying on as normal."

"I wouldn't close. I can keep the place running if you don't feel up to it, because as soon as people hear about this, they'll want to drop in here and chat about Rob. It's a real thing that Fairview does. At first, I thought it was just to do with gossiping, but then I saw how it helped. Getting together and sharing stories about a person who lived here all his life is good for the soul."

The lump in Lyra's throat grew again so that she had to force out the words. "In that case, we should stay open and start cooking before the breakfast rush arrives. Can I fix you something, Dan?"

"I don't think I could eat right now, but I wouldn't mind more coffee."

Lyra's stomach churned as she imagined his did. It was hard to accept that Rob was gone. She would miss him and his gentle teasing. "Help yourself to coffee and anything else and stay here for as long as you like. Don't bother with work today—I insist."

He didn't answer and appeared to be fighting back tears. Her heart ached for him. In her old life, Dan had been her driver and filled in with personal security if required. When she'd left LA, the transition was so much easier because Dan and Maggie opted to come with her to live and work in Portland. None of them anticipated the move to Fairview, but those two readily agreed when the idea came up.

Seemingly content with their decision, Lyra was grateful to have good friends beside her to share the adventure. With Leroy, Poppy, and Earl, this place ran well enough and gave Lyra time out to work on her recipes with Maggie. They were like one big family, and Rob had slotted right in.

A diner was hard work and nothing like running a fancy restaurant like the one in LA, but she loved having more contact with her customers, and to be cooking every day once more filled her with joy.

Fancy cooking was great, and she was proud of her success, but it was stressful, and being famous had never appealed to Lyra. Once the gilt wore off her celebrity status in Fairview, she simply became Lyra from the diner, cooking meals that any family would eat. Which suited her just fine.

Now Dan would come back to live with her and Maggie, which wasn't a problem. In between remodeling the diner, he'd fixed up two bedrooms in the old farmhouse out the back and had begun on another. Maggie lived in one of the rooms, and Lyra had the master bedroom. Dan would have to take another room that was far from finished. She knew he wouldn't mind that, only the reason for it coming about.

Of course, Lyra's mom was due home from her cruise in a couple of weeks, which might be an issue, but she wouldn't worry about that for now.

There was also the matter of Dan and Maggie being under the same roof again. Would it make things awkward now that they were seeing so much of each other? Lyra sighed. That was also something to worry about later. Right now, she had to stop herself from crying and get on with cooking.

They cooked the usual fare found in diners across the country. Plus, Lyra added a couple of more upmarket meals each week and swapped them around. Customers had their favorites but had become surprisingly eager to try something new.

Of course her mind was in turmoil and finding other things to worry about to stop her thinking about Rob. This was a good thing because there was work to do. Today she was making tortellini. Little parcels of chicken that almost melted in your mouth were proving very popular. They were fiddly and had to be made as ordered, but the filling could be made well ahead of time, and this is what she started as soon as she'd put the bread in the industrial oven to bake.

Finely chopping the onion brought tears to her eyes. Only when she got to the other vegetables the tears got heavier and when she got to the chicken she stifled a sob. In the bathroom she allowed the tears to flow, the image of Rob dying alone too much to bear. Slowly, noises from the kitchen pulled her out of her melancholy enough to remember that the younger members of staff would arrive soon.

Poppy and Earl were inclined to be curious about most things which was usually a good thing. Today their curiosity would be hard to deal with and their sadness even harder.

As far as she and Dan knew, his health prior to today or last night had been fine. Except for that tiredness. Poppy, Earl, and Leroy would also be upset to hear that Rob obviously hadn't been well. In fact, Lyra felt guilty that she hadn't suspected and therefore not paid enough attention to his health. If she had known, she might have been able to help.

6

By lunchtime the diner was full inside and out, and people hung around the front door waiting for seats to empty. No one wanted to leave, and it was all because of Rob.

Arabelle walked in at her usual time, and the noisy chatter stopped. She stalled halfway across the room and looked about her suspiciously. She had everyone's attention, and by the scowl she didn't like it one bit.

"What's going on? Do I have something on my face?" she asked the room at large.

Lyra stepped around the counter and made her way through the crowd. "Arabelle, would you come into the kitchen for a moment?"

"Why on earth would I do that?"

"I have something important to tell you."

Arabelle's eyes narrowed. "Something everyone else already knows?"

Lyra nodded, expecting the woman to refuse again, but she didn't.

"This is very odd." Arabelle hesitated, looked around her

once more, and ushered Lyra ahead of her. "Very well but make it quick so I can get out of this zoo."

Lyra led her to the large table in the kitchen. From over at the grill, Leroy raised an eyebrow, but continued cooking.

"Would you like to take a seat?"

Arabelle sniffed. "I'm not fond of theatrics, so if you don't mind, I'll stand while you get whatever it is off your chest."

"Very well." Lyra clasped her hands in front of her white apron. "Ms. Filmore, I'm sorry to say that Rob McKenna died late last night."

Arabelle's eye narrowed. "That's not a very nice thing to joke about."

"I'm afraid it's no joke," Lyra said softly. "Dan found him first thing."

Arabelle tucked her bag firmly around her arm at the elbow and looked out the window. "While that is unfortunate, it's no concern of mine. The old goat ate the rubbish you fed him without a fuss. I daresay he brought this on himself."

Lyra gasped, but Arabelle simply turned and stalked out of the kitchen, and the diner, without a backward glance. Curious looks from the other customers were directed at the kitchen. Lyra turned to Leroy, who had witnessed the scene. "She's blaming us," she said quietly, when what she really wanted was to yell after Arabelle how despicable she was.

"Sounded that way." Leroy shrugged. "Don't pay her no mind. The woman's as caustic as disinfectant."

"Has she always been that way?"

He plated up chicken soup and garlic bread. "I heard tell she was nice once upon a time, but she had a bad love experience."

"Arabelle was in love?"

"Sure." He nodded enthusiastically. "Love isn't just for the sweet and innocent."

Lyra blushed. "I didn't mean to imply that it wasn't. It's just that she doesn't seem to like anybody."

"Some people are born bad, but others become who they are through life lessons. I guess her lessons weren't good. That experience might be reason enough to turn her into someone who can no longer see the good in anyone."

Lyra nodded. She'd met a few people like that over the years. Her ex-agent in particular had been full of good intentions when they first met. Or he'd pretended to be. Once she became famous, he'd turned into someone she couldn't bear to be associated with.

Poppy poked her head around the doorway. The poor girl had been upset all morning, refusing to go home, but now she was angry. "She's gone and didn't stop for her tea. Just stomped out through everyone like a knife through butter."

"Guess you'd better go say something," Leroy suggested.

It took a moment for Lyra to realize that he was talking to her. "Me? Why do I have to say anything? We're not at his funeral."

"It's your diner, and Rob loved it. Just a few words, then they'll go about their business. People in small towns need a little push, otherwise they'll be talking in there all day. Unless that doesn't worry you." He nodded at the sound of raised voices.

Lyra went back into the diner to find four women arguing about seating. Two were seated and another two wanted those seats. Now.

"Excuse me, everyone."

All faces turned her way, and most people stopped talking. She licked her lips and tried to find the right words. "This is a very sad day. We were all fond of Rob, and when we find out about his arrangements, you can be sure that the diner will help with the catering. Meanwhile, we can only have a certain number of people in here at one time. If you're

47

done eating, we'd appreciate you moving on so others can order. We're also happy to put your food in takeaway containers."

Dan appeared at the front door and held it open, looking pointedly at a large group spread over several tables who'd been there since opening a couple of hours ago. His size gave him a measure of authority, and the group departed with mostly good grace.

Poppy bustled around the crowd to quickly clean tables even as the two women threw themselves at the empty seats. Lyra sighed. The small win was welcome, but the battle still simmered.

The door opened again, and the sheriff entered. Removing his hat, he nodded to everyone on his way to the counter. "Ms. St. Claire, I'd like a word. In private."

"Of course." Lyra went through the doorway into the kitchen, and he followed. Leroy was at the grill, but over by the table was probably the best she could do in terms of privacy. "Do you know any more about Rob? Was it a heart attack?"

The sheriff studied her for a moment before taking out a pad and pen from his shirt pocket. "I have no information for you, but perhaps you have something to tell me about Mr. McKenna?"

His manner was gruff, and the few times they'd met around town, he'd been the same. She couldn't think what she might have done to have him treat her this way, and it bugged her. More than it should, which bugged her some more.

Lyra appreciated that he would want to know Rob's whereabouts if there'd been foul play, but if it was death by heart attack, then this line of questioning wasn't necessary. It didn't take a detective to work that out.

"I'm not sure what you're asking."

He tapped the pad impatiently. "Let's start with his whereabouts yesterday."

"He came to the diner last night for his dinner, but I didn't see him after he'd eaten."

"And what did that meal consist of?"

"Steak with all the trimmings." She couldn't help the terseness. *Where the heck was he going with this? If it was to suggest she had poisoned him...*

"I believe he had an altercation with Ms. Filmore."

Lyra gaped. "Surely, you don't suspect Arabelle of killing Rob?"

"I'm not suggesting anything. Was there an altercation or not?"

"Sort of," she admitted. "That was early in the morning though."

He wrote a couple of words, turning the pad away when he noticed her interest. "Please tell me what they argued about."

"They often bickered, so it wasn't unusual. This time Rob told her to hurry up with ordering, then teased her about her name which she wasn't happy about. She basically called him overweight. It was all a bit silly really."

"I'll be the judge of that."

Lyra bristled at his tone. "That's all that happened, so I don't know what else you want me to say."

"Do you know how to do CPR?"

This was unexpected, and Lyra's stomach clenched at why he needed to know. "I did a course a few years back."

He raised an eyebrow. "What about your employees—in or out of the diner?"

She didn't like this at all. "Everyone I employ has done a course. Why is this important?"

The sheriff merely wrote a few more notes. "Do you have any knowledge about herbs?"

She raised an eyebrow. "I'm a chef."

He simply stared, which flustered her.

"I meant that I cook with herbs every day."

"Do you use them in any other way that might be medicinal?"

A red light flashed in her mind. Now she was certain the sheriff meant that Rob was poisoned. "Never. Even my herbal teas are store-bought."

"Did Mr. McKenna argue with anyone else?"

"Not that I ever saw. He was a lovely man who seemed well-liked by everyone else. In the time I knew him, he never had a cross word to say about anyone. Except Ms. Filmore."

He snapped his notebook shut. "Thank you. That will be all."

She frowned at his dismissal. "Then I can get back to work?"

He looked around them as if he'd forgotten where they were and that Lyra wasn't going anywhere. He nodded and hastily headed back into the diner.

She hoped he wasn't going to question her customers right now because it would take a very long time to get through them all and had the potential to become some sort of sideshow. Amongst all this she recalled what Rob had said two days ago. *A person who turns on a tap isn't likely bent on physically hurting another.* Was he wrong about that?

Leroy dropped bacon on the grill. "Sounds to me like he was helped over the rainbow."

Lyra had forgotten he was there. "Pardon?"

"Rob. Sounds like someone killed him."

She gulped. "With the sheriff asking questions about arguments, it certainly makes you think so. I wonder who he suspects. Someone who knows CPR? But why would that factor into things if he was murdered?" Lyra shivered.

"Unless the person changed their mind. I guess we won't know anything until an autopsy's been done."

Leroy's spatula hung in mid-air until he clanged it onto the grill. "Are they doing an autopsy?"

"If there is any doubt of how he died, they will."

"I guess that's true." He flipped the bacon and patties thoughtfully. "Anyway, unless he's got questions, the sheriff's pretty closemouthed about things happening in his town, so I wouldn't count on hearing one way or the other for a while."

Lyra meant it sincerely when she said what a great guy Rob was and how much she thought of him, which meant she had to know what actually killed him.

And Leroy was right about the sheriff keeping things close to his chest. He'd certainly not shared any information after she'd asked him to investigate the business of the flooding. Lyra got the impression by his distant manner around her that he didn't trust her. Therefore, he was hardly likely to tell her anything about Rob's death. Which meant if Rob really had been the victim of foul play, the only way she would discover who was responsible was if she asked her own questions.

And, she had to know if he had family to ensure a decent send-off. At the very least, Rob deserved that.

It was also true that keeping busy would prevent her from falling to pieces.

7

A pparently, the sheriff was indeed talking to several people about Rob's whereabouts the night he died. He'd also spoken to her staff one at a time, including Dan for a second time. Each of them was left upset and in some cases scared.

She commiserated as much as she could, but eventually Lyra used the excuse of needing a few grocery items to get out of the diner and away from all the gossip. The knitting group in particular was relentless. If she got asked one more time about the sheriff treating Rob's death as suspicious and what that might mean, she would scream.

With Cinnamon at her heels, she walked down Main Street, the sunshine at odds with the sadness in her heart that Rob would never join her again. The three of them had mainly walked around town in the late afternoons. Since Rob knew every person they met, it was more of a stroll.

He'd introduced her to people she'd never seen in the diner, as well as some whose names she couldn't remember. When that was the case, he'd whisper out of the corner of his mouth so she could greet them properly and often threw out a snippet such as how many children they had or what they were known for in the community.

At each meeting he also introduced Cinnamon and then mentioned the diner, crowing over a particular item on the menu. It made her laugh that it was never the same thing. He was a great ambassador for the Beagle Diner, but she would sorely miss having him around in every capacity. And so would Cinnamon.

Lost in fond memories of her friend, Lyra would have walked on by when the regular bus pulled up outside the library, but something drew her eye. An elegant woman with red hair disembarked and glanced up the street. This was unexpected, as was the yearning for something she hadn't realized was missing stole over her.

"Mom!" Lyra called.

"Lyra!" Patricia St. Claire swung around and enveloped Lyra in a firm hug. "How wonderful to see your beautiful face the minute I arrive."

With her mom's head tucked under her chin, Lyra's heart expanded, while Cinnamon danced between them, her tail thumping their legs.

"Hello, Cinnamon. Are you enjoying your new home?"

The beagle yipped and dropped onto her back, expecting a belly rub.

"What are you doing here, and why are you on a bus?" Lyra asked, her mind already trying to work out where her mom would sleep tonight.

Holding her at arm's length, Patricia searched Lyra's face. "Aren't you pleased to see me?"

"Of course, but you should have told me you were arriving today. I would have organized to pick you up from the airport."

"My darling girl, I know you must be exhausting your

cash supplies by now with the sale of my apartment not going through. Did you forget that we didn't grow up rich and I am perfectly capable of making my own way home?"

"Well, no, but you haven't taken a bus in years."

Patricia bent over the prancing beagle. "And I thoroughly enjoyed the experience, didn't I, Cinnamon?"

The beagle squirmed in delight, making sounds of agreement as the bus driver placed two suitcases on the pavement.

"Here you go, Mrs. St. Claire."

"Why, thank you, Brack. It's been a pleasure to ride with you."

Patricia placed a folded bill into the hand she shook, and Lyra smiled. Her mom might be "roughing it," but she'd developed a few habits she couldn't shake. Patricia waved out to the other passengers, which didn't surprise Lyra at all. Her mom made friends easily, and people were drawn to her bubbly personality.

Several gaped at Lyra through the windows, and she gave a friendly wave, pleased that her mom had obviously managed to keep their connection to herself. After telling many of them to keep in touch, Patricia was finally ready. Lyra pulled at the handles of the trolley cases, which rolled easily enough along the walk.

Patricia reached out. "Let me take one."

"I've got them," Lyra insisted, having noticed the tiredness in her mom's eyes and that she'd lost quite a bit of weight. "It's not far, and I can't wait to get home and show you what we've done to the place." Lyra headed in the direction of the diner, which they would pass on the way to the house.

Patricia stopped outside the diner and peered through the window. "Aren't we going in here first? It already looks so different from when we lived here. Your touches make it so much more attractive, and I'd love to see the rest of it."

People stared out at them, and Lyra barely hesitated. She

wanted a private place to tell her about Rob before someone else did. "Can we drop the bags off first? You'll have as much time as you like to look around once you're settled, and I have to get back to work."

Patricia hesitated. "I hope my early arrival won't put you out too much."

"Not at all," Lyra assured her. "I'm so glad you're here. If it didn't sound that way, it's only because I wanted your bedroom to be finished, but you can have mine until it is."

"I'll sleep wherever is convenient. It certainly doesn't have to be fancy, and I don't want to kick you out of your room." There was a small silence, as they walked on to the corner, before Mom continued. "To be honest, I'd had enough of holidaying by myself. I got quite lonely. Even with so many nice people in my group."

It hung in the air that until a few months ago Mom was in a relationship. The man in question sold Lyra's itinerary and whereabouts to the paparazzi. More than once. During a rash of unsolved murder and arson. While she was glad that Mom finished with him, there was no way she wanted her to be sad.

Stopping in the driveway, Lyra turned. "Then I'm glad you decided to cut it short. You certainly won't be lonely here. Plus, I could use an extra pair of hands, if you feel up to it?"

Mom pulled a tissue from her handbag and dabbed her eyes. "It's a relief to hear you say that. I wasn't sure if you really wanted me to come to Fairview, and part of me wondered if you'd find me an apartment somewhere where I wouldn't be a bother. It will be wonderful to be needed again."

Lyra gasped and pulled her mom into her arms. "How could you think that I don't need you in my life? I was worried that you'd feel as though I was dragging you around the country again without giving you a choice about where you could live."

"We're a fine pair." Patricia hiccupped. "I'm not sure how life got so complicated."

"Me either." Lyra shrugged. "But I'm glad we got that sorted. Come on, I bet you'd love some coffee." They got to the wide steps, and Lyra manhandled the bags onto the porch. She opened the door with a flourish and stood back. "What do you think?"

Patricia's hands clasped her neck while she took in everything. "Oh my. From the outside it looks the same, only very tired, but in here, it's just beautiful."

Lyra smiled happily, enjoying seeing the place though fresh eyes. "It's a lot different from when we lived here. I hope you don't mind the changes."

"Not at all. It's a hundred times better. We never had the money to do much, but even if we had, I would never have the vision to do all this." Her hand waved around the room. "The open plan is perfect and lets in so much light."

"That was the plan. Although, I can't take all the credit. I told her what I needed, but Maggie designed everything and advised me on colors."

"Then I shall tell her what a fantastic job she's done as well."

Lyra ran her hand over the stone countertop, picturing the old wooden one and her family squeezed into the small kitchen, jostling good-naturedly for space. "We were so happy here, weren't we?"

Patricia nodded, her eyes glistening once more. "Until you moved away, I couldn't imagine living anywhere else. They were the best days of my life. It will always be that way because your father and I were born here and it's where we raised you. I still miss him, you know."

A tightness gripped Lyra's chest. "Me too."

"Your dad was so proud of you. Imagine how he'd feel to see how well you've done."

Lyra grimaced. "I lost the restaurant that was my proudest achievement, but I like to think he'd be happy that I came home."

Patricia waved a finger. "Your agent let you down and left you afraid when he should have supported and taken care of you, which is what he promised me. Then your accountant stole your money to take care of her father. Trusting someone is never a failure, even when it's misguided. Besides, you could have prosecuted Lisa, and you didn't because you could see she needed the money more than you did. You work harder than anyone I know, so don't ever talk yourself down and be proud of what you still have. I am, more than I can say."

The heartfelt words made Lyra's chin quiver. "Thanks, Mom. I needed to hear that."

Patricia patted her hand. "I should have said it more often. Now, I can't wait to become reacquainted with some of my friends. I do hope they'll forgive me for not staying in touch the way I promised."

This was as good a time as any to talk about Rob. "About that. I have some sad news."

Patricia's eyes widened. "Is it Martha?"

Lyra didn't prolong the fear. "Martha's fine. Rob McKenna passed away yesterday."

Patricia dropped onto a chair. "Oh no. That really is sad. I saw his house as we walked by and wondered how things were for him these days. He was the first person on my to-visit list after Martha."

Cinnamon put her nose on Patricia's lap and looked up at her with soulful eyes. Mom absently scratched between the twitching ears.

"Rob spoke of you and Dad and how fond he was of the two of you," Lyra said gently. "Like I told you on the phone, he helped us out so much when we arrived. From giving Dan a hand with the renovations, advising us on where to get the best deals for building materials, and suggestions for people to hire, he made everything a darn sight easier than if we'd tackled everything by ourselves."

"That sounds like Rob." Patricia gave a watery smile. "He was always generous and knew every man, woman, and pet for miles around."

"You knew him well, right?"

"Very well." Patricia stared wistfully at the house next door. "Rob and your father were the best of friends, and he spent a lot of time in this house."

"Can I ask about his life? Only, I couldn't remember him being married or having kids."

"It's a tragic story which kept Rob down for many years." Patricia sighed. "His wife, Dahlia, died young from a heart problem. They had one son, Phillip, who was poorly most of his young life with the same congenital disease. After Dahlia passed on, her parents stepped in and took the boy to live with them. Rob didn't want that because they lived so far away, but he had his business to run, and the boy did need a lot of care. He saw him whenever he could, but as far as we could tell, the parents turned the boy against his father."

"That's awful."

Patricia nodded. "It truly was. Rob tried to get him back several times, but the boy got upset about being uprooted again and refused. It almost broke Rob when, after a huge argument, his son wouldn't come visit at all. Rob didn't have the heart to force him by taking his wife's parents to court and potentially making his boy hate him. He hoped it would change as the child got older, but it never did, and eventually there was no contact at all. His letters came back return to sender and the phone number was disconnected. He did get at least one letter from the in-law's solicitor asking him to desist, as it was causing the boy stress. From that time until we left town, he didn't even have a current photo of his son."

Shocked, Lyra reached for a tissue and handed the box to her mom. "I remember Rob from before I left, but how did I not know this about his family?"

"You weren't born when it all began, and Rob was a private man. After a while he never mentioned them to anyone and shut down any conversation about his son." Patricia sniffed. "You have to understand that it wasn't because he didn't care—it just hurt too much."

Lyra could appreciate this way of dealing with things. It was the kind of self-preservation she'd employed once or twice in her old life. *But what about now?* She couldn't bear it if Rob didn't have the funeral he deserved. "Do you think his son will organize the funeral?"

"I'd imagine so. He had no other family that I know of."

Lyra shook her head. "I guess the police or funeral home will chase that up, but what if no one comes to take care of things?"

"Then I'll step up," Patricia said firmly. "And those that want to can help."

"You've no idea how much that puts my mind at rest." Lyra breathed a sigh of relief. "I'm so glad you're here, Mom, and if you do end up managing the funeral, the diner will contribute whatever you need to make it awesome."

They hugged again, then Patricia stood. "I can unpack anytime. What I'd really like is to see this diner I've heard so much about."

Lyra grinned. "It's not the fancy restaurant you're used to, but I love it."

"Which is the most important thing of all. Fancy has its

place, but nothing beats a good meal cooked with love, and you can only get that where it lives."

Mom was right. The food she cooked these days was so much plainer, but it was still cooked with the same amount of effort and love. Arm in arm, they headed out the door followed by one happy beagle.

8

_____

"Sorry I've been gone so long." Lyra stepped through the kitchen doorway and moved to the left so her mom could get by. "Look who I found."

"Mrs. St. Claire!" Maggie jumped up from the table and came to hug Patricia. "You look fabulous and so tanned."

"Thank you, dear. I've had a lovely time, but I needed to see my girl."

Cinnamon yipped from the doorway.

Patricia laughed. "Make that my *girls*. Goodness, look at this kitchen."

"It's nowhere near the size of La Joliesse, but it is every bit as functional." Lyra hoped she didn't sound as defensive as she felt over the considerable differences, but Mom simply nodded and Lyra continued the tour. "This is Leroy. He's the head chef and makes the best omelets. His burgers are amazing too."

Leroy laughed. "Your daughter is far too kind. Nothing I make can compare with Lyra's cooking."

"Pleased to meet you Leroy, and if Lyra says you're good

at cooking something you can bet that it's true. She never lies about food."

He gave a small bow and, with a grin, turned back to his pot of soup.

"Come and see the diner, Mom. There's bound to be someone you know there."

There were quite a few customers, and again Lyra moved away to let her mom get the whole picture of the revamped diner. "Hello, everyone," Lyra called out to gain their attention, and grinned when Mom entered the room as if she were on a red carpet.

Martha Curran, wearing a kaftan, hurried across the room to hug her. "Patricia! We've been wondering when you'd turn up. June thought she saw you outside, but I took a look and, well, it doesn't matter. You're here at last!"

"I just got in and couldn't wait to catch up with you all. I love the brown bob."

Martha preened. "It was time for a change."

"I see you're all still knitting up a storm. I might get into it again once I'm settled. Where's Vanessa Fife?"

"Our leader's at the bank, but she'll be in soon." Martha rolled her eyes, and they both laughed.

"We hear you've been off cruising." Tall and thin, with steel-gray hair, June Edmonson called across the room. "You have to tell us all about it. We've been dying to know if it's as great as it looks on TV."

Patricia laughed and joined them at the table for a round of hugs. "It's just like you see on the movies. Parts of it are even better. There's never a dull moment if you have a hankering for some fun. And, if you want to relax, you can sit and do nothing. Don't get me started on the food. There's a buffet running pretty much all day long. They just change out the type of foods depending on the time of day, or if they have a theme running."

"Any nice men aboard?"

"Plenty, Carrie-Ann." Patricia sniffed. "If a person was interested, which I certainly was not."

"Oh, yes. You had that debacle with your boyfriend selling information about Lyra. Good on you for getting rid of him!"

Patricia's mouth pinched for the briefest of moments, then her eyes twinkled at Martha. "No one hurts my daughter and gets away with it. Now, tell me everything that's happened around here since I left."

Martha shrugged. "Sure, if you want to be bored. Fairview can't possibly compete with the life you've had. Living in LA must have been incredibly exciting."

"It was for a while, but all that glitz and glitter gets tiresome. Frankly, I'm looking forward to relaxing and being around family and friends."

"So, you didn't make any new friends?" Martha asked coyly.

"I met some nice people, but no one could compare to the ones I left here. I'm so sorry I didn't keep in touch as often as I intended to. Every time we talked, it made me homesick."

Patricia said this quietly, but Lyra heard and had another pang of guilt. She had no idea this was how her mom felt.

Martha dabbed at her eyes. "Never mind. You're back now, and that's all that matters, right, girls?"

"We've been counting the days until we could see you," Carrie-Ann agreed.

"How lovely. Although, it would have been a better homecoming, but for Rob no longer being with us."

"Oh, my goodness, it's so tragic!" Martha sniffed. "We only saw him the day before, and he was fine."

By now, a few other women stood near, and they all began talking at once. Despite the sadness over Rob, Mom looked to be enjoying herself, so Lyra left her to catch up.

"Order up," Leroy called.

Poppy was busy cleaning tables, so Lyra took the plate out herself. Working in restaurants for so long, she wasn't without skills as a waitress. The customer sat at a table for two in the corner, his eyes on the group of women who had rejoined the table opposite him along with Patricia.

"Here you are. Rare steak, fries, and salad."

He was middle-aged, with a slim build and dark-hair, and when he looked up, he seemed familiar.

"Thank you." He moved the plate to the left and right, studying it from every angle.

From experience she got that he wasn't so much checking the standard of the food as critiquing Lyra St. Claire, celebrity chef. She forced a smile. "Can I get you anything else?"

He thought for a second. "Do you know where I can find a man called Daniel Best?"

This wasn't the question she expected. "Dan's in Destiny." She checked her watch. "But he'll be back in the next hour."

"Back where exactly?"

"He's working on my house which is behind the diner, Mr....?"

He stared for a heartbeat or two. "McKenna."

The penny dropped. Those eyes and shape of his face—it was now so obvious. "You're Rob's son?"

"That's right. You knew him?"

"Of course. Everyone knows Rob."

His eyes narrowed. "From what I hear, you're new to town."

Clearly, he did know who she was. "I was born here, and we lived next door to your father for years before we moved away. It was nice to be neighbors again. We will miss him."

Now his eyes widened, which told her a lot. Such as, he wasn't a true follower of hers and was only interested in her recent history. He'd made assumptions about how she got here, the way so many people did.

"I wish I could say the same." He coughed as if he'd said too much. "This Dan—Dad liked him?"

"Very much. With your father's help, Dan remodeled and refurbished the diner, my house, and did a few renovations for your dad in between. The last two are ongoing." How she wished he'd be around to finish them. It would mean this was all a bad dream.

"Sounds like a peach of a guy."

The bitterness was unmistakable, and Lyra bristled. "They both are."

"Were," he stated flatly and picked up his knife and fork.

The dismissal rankled, yet she wanted to be charitable. Not everyone reacted the same when a family member died. "I'm sorry for your loss, and if you want to talk about your dad, anytime, I'm usually found in the kitchen here or at my house." When she turned, Lyra felt his eyes on her back. She'd bet a cupcake or two that behind those dark eyes were equally dark secrets and sadness. It was a shame that Rob and his son never reunited. No matter the reason, both men had obviously been hurt by the separation. Or was she seeing things that didn't exist?

Back at her usual place in a corner of the kitchen with her laptop, Maggie looked up when Lyra entered. She was about to tell her about the meeting, but Patricia hurried after her.

"What was that all about? You look upset."

Lyra spoke quietly. "You won't believe who that customer is. I get the feeling that he doesn't want anyone to know he's here, but that's Rob's son."

Patricia peeked into the diner. "My, he's changed significantly. He used to look more like his mom, and now I can see Rob in him. The poor boy. After all these years, I should introduce myself and offer my assistance with the arrangements."

Lyra put a hand on her arm. "He seems a bit uptight. I'd let him be just now while he finishes his meal. Then perhaps it would be better if I tell him that you're offering."

"Why can't I talk to him?" Patricia stiffened. "Do you think I'd say something wrong?"

Lyra's cheeks burned, and all words stuck in her throat.

Patricia gasped. "You do! Well, that's nice, isn't it?"

A touch of panic caused Lyra to blurt out, "I know you'd never intend to upset him, but he's a little testy. Think how he feels about organizing a funeral for a man who's all but a stranger."

Patricia fussed with a pile of napkins. "It will be difficult, which is why I want to help."

"And he'll likely jump at the offer given a bit more time to come to terms with things. We don't want him to think that we're all talking about him behind his back."

A delicate eyebrow shot up. "The way I did with Archie?"

This was awkward. Mom telling her boyfriend of Lyra's plans and him leaking them to the press wasn't something she ever intended to bring up again, especially since Mom was no longer with him. "That's not what I meant."

"Maybe not consciously," Patricia huffed. "I think it's time I went and unpacked."

"Please don't take offense," Lyra pleaded.

"Why would I?" Patricia walked out the back door, her shoulders slightly stooped.

Cinnamon gave Lyra a quizzical look and followed Patricia. At least one of them was able to offer support, since Lyra couldn't keep her big foot out of her mouth.

"Darn it. She was enjoying herself until now. Why did I have to stop her?"

Maggie poured a large mug of coffee and thrust it into Lyra's hand. "Because you care about a stranger."

Lyra's lips pursed. "Mom's feelings should come first."

"She'll get over it the way she always does when she sees your point of view."

Lyra stared at Maggie and carefully placed the mug on the table. "Have I been such an awful daughter?"

"What? Don't be ridiculous."

"But if that's how you see us—Mom always having to back down—that's just not right."

Maggie grimaced. "Sometimes I say stuff without thinking about how it sounds."

"Not very often, and you always speak the truth." Lyra sighed. "I obviously need to apologize to Mom some more. A lot more."

"Okay, but maybe you should first tell Dan that Rob's son is here." Maggie nodded at the window. "Although, you may be too late."

Lyra checked, and through the hedge she saw Dan's car in the driveway over at the house. He leaned on the hood chatting with Patricia. "I'll give them a minute to talk, so she doesn't think I'm interfering between her and Dan as well."

"You're learning," Leroy muttered.

It seemed even he thought she hadn't been fair on Mom.

Just then, Poppy returned to the kitchen with a large plate. "The guy who had the steak asked me to tell you that it was pretty good. I didn't hurt him for such a casual remark because he left a large tip."

Leroy laughed. "He probably thought Lyra made it."

"I have no idea how to take that," Lyra mused. "Did he already leave? I wanted to talk to him."

Poppy nodded and rinsed the plate and cutlery then loaded them into the industrial dishwasher. "He turned right out the door if that helps."

Lyra removed the apron she hadn't long put on. "Earl should be here soon, and I'll be at the farmhouse if you need me." She hurried out the door, keeping an eye on Rob's house. If that's where he'd gone, then he must be inside, so she went in search of Dan who was no longer by his car. Voices led her to where he stood on the back deck which overlooked the stream, with Mom beside him.

Dan turned when he heard her. "Patricia told me that Rob's son is here."

Lyra nodded "He wants to talk to you."

"I wonder what about. I moved everything of mine out, so how did he even know I lived there?"

Lyra snorted. "I don't know how long he's been in town, but I daresay a well-meaning resident told him. Anyway, I'm pretty sure he's at Rob's place now."

He ran his fingers through his hair. "I guess if he's asking after me, I should go find out why."

They watched him walk through the house, slower than she'd ever seen him move.

Patricia turned to face her. "I hope you don't mind me telling Dan about Rob's son."

"Of course not. He had to know. I guess they'll talk about Rob. What do you think about him turning up like this?"

"What do you mean?"

"Rob just died, and now his son's here. It seems very fast to me. I guess the sheriff must have tracked him down and he got an immediate flight. Or maybe he lives close."

"That sounds logical. Although, it would be a shame if he did live close by and hadn't come to see Rob." Patricia tilted her head. "You wanted to go with Dan to find out, didn't you?

"No…" Lyra shrugged. "Maybe I did."

"Hah! After all you said, you want to know the why of things, which makes you no different to me."

Initially Lyra stiffened, but a laugh bubbled up. "You know what? I can't think of anyone else I'd rather be more like."

"Really?" Patricia sniffed. "I thought maybe you'd changed your mind about having me live with you. I don't want to be a bother."

"Please don't ever think that." Lyra hugged her. "I hate to see you upset over my thoughtlessness. Ignore everything I've said, and I'm sorry if I've been neglectful or bossy."

Patricia squeezed hard. "Darling, don't take that on your shoulders. I'm probably overly sensitive right now. Being back where your dad's presence is as strong as ever, is making me sentimental and weepy, but I promise, you never forced me to do anything or go anywhere. I made those decisions."

"But you felt like you should move so you could be near me, right?"

Patricia sniffed again. "Still my choice. You deserve to have the life that will make you happy, and there was no reason for me to stay in Fairview and certainly not in LA if you weren't there."

"But I made a mess of things that caused you to pull up stakes twice when we had so little time together."

"Not from where I'm sitting. You took chances and did amazing things. So, what if you don't own a fancy restaurant. The diner is a credit to you, and I can see that you're happier here than you've been in a long while."

"Thanks, Mom. You always were my biggest cheerleader."

"When you wait as long as we did to have a child, they become your focus. Your father felt the same. He would have walked the world to be near you, and I feel closer to him here."

"Me too." Tears coursed down Lyra's cheeks, and she

welcomed another hug. "For the record, I don't blame you for what Archie did."

"I'm so glad. He was a schmuck, and I have no idea what I saw in him except he was company. Look at us." Patricia leaned back and shook her head. "What a fine pair. We're back together in our wonderful town. That's a reason to smile and not worry about the past."

Lyra laughed through her tears. The loss of Rob was the only real reason to be sad right now.

9

Lyra and her mom were sitting at the counter going through photos of the cruise when Dan stormed into the house.

"Rob's son is a fool!"

In the years that she'd known him, Lyra had never seen him this upset. "What's wrong?"

"He accused me of living with his father to trick him into leaving me his possessions."

"No way!"

"It's true and absolutely ridiculous to believe Rob would do any such thing. I just can't understand how he came to his conclusions. He started out all casual as you please, then the conversation got darker. He questioned everything I did during my stay there. It was frustrating, but I was totally honest about what I did around the house, that I wasn't paid, and how Rob refused to take any rent even though I offered many times. I'd hardly finished when he hits me with taking advantage and intimated that I'm a liar and a thief."

"I've a good mind to speak to him," Patricia said through pursed lips. "And tell him how wrong and unkind he's being."

"There's no point. He won't listen to reason no matter what anyone says. The guy's got a belly full of anger, and it's spewing out of him like lava. I guess I'm the easiest target."

"Why would he come to town, guns blazing?" Lyra was also riled up. "He doesn't know anything about you or Rob."

"Let's remember he just lost his father, no matter that they were estranged." Patricia was the first to calm down and spoke soothingly. "Perhaps he feels bad that he can't make amends."

"He's a bit too old to be acting out," Dan muttered as he slumped in a chair.

A knock on the door was almost a relief, and Lyra jumped up. "I'll get it."

The sheriff and another police officer stood on the porch looking very serious.

Sheriff Walker removed his hat. "Good morning, Ms. St. Claire. Is Daniel Best here?"

Lyra frowned at the full name usage. This visit didn't bode well. "Dan's inside. Please come in."

Dan stood as soon as he saw them. "What's happened now?"

That got Sheriff Walker's attention quicker than a new item on the menu. "Why do you ask, Mr. Best?"

The casual tone didn't fool Lyra, but Dan didn't appear to read more into the question.

"Because I've just had a run-in with Phillip McKenna, and he threatened me."

"In what way?"

"He said I would get what I deserved."

The sheriff frowned. "What exactly were you arguing about?"

Dan ran his fingers through his buzz cut hair, a hangover from his army days. "He said I took advantage of his father, which just isn't true. I worked around his house in my spare time, and yes, I lived there rent free, but it was a win-win situation because we enjoyed each other's company and I never charged for any of the materials I used."

Something in the way the sheriff nodded as he listened seemed strange to Lyra. "But you know all this, Sheriff Walker, don't you?"

He shuffled his feet and, apart from a brief irate glance at her, continued his questioning. "Obviously, we don't know every detail of your conversation, but Mr. McKenna told us that you talked Rob into signing over his garage to you."

"He did what?" Dan dropped back into the chair behind him. "That can't be right."

"Until the will is read, there's no way of being sure, but this is what Mr. McKenna believes."

Lyra frowned. "But how could he know, if he has no official word, what is in the will?"

"It appears that his dad wrote to him and asked him to come to Fairview. When his son didn't reply, he sent another letter outlining his will and asking again if he could come so they could talk things over."

Patricia gasped. "Did Rob know he would die soon?"

"That's not for me to say." The sheriff turned back to Dan. "Naturally, we'll verify everything, and you should receive a letter from Rob's solicitor, Karl Lowe, very soon."

"So, you've spoken with Karl already?" Lyra asked.

Sheriff Walker did that shoe shuffle thing again. "We did happen to see him before we came here, but we have no documents to prove anything. Mr. McKenna didn't bring the letters with him, so we're merely here to discuss if there was anything we should be aware of that occurred between you and Rob. Knowing sooner rather than later would be better."

Dan spoke through gritted teeth. "There was only ever

mutual respect, and as I said, enjoyment of each other's company."

"I can vouch for Dan," Lyra interjected before he let off the steam that was threatening to explode "He's done amazing things here and at Rob's place. You only have to look around both houses to see how hard he works, and Rob often complained to me that Dan would never take compensation."

"But you pay him?" the sheriff needled.

"Yes, I hired him years ago, and unless I'm mistaken, that's the way employment works." With an effort, she dialed back the sarcasm. "As Dan already said, what he did for Rob was in exchange for a roof over his head—in lieu of any payment. But it went beyond that because they were friends and Dan helps his friends. That's the kind of man he is and certainly not the man Phillip McKenna is attempting to portray him as."

The sheriff tucked his notebook into his shirt pocket. "Well, I think that's all for now. We'll be in touch if we have any further questions. Meanwhile, please advise us if you remember anything else we ought to know. You should also remain in town for the next few days."

"Just Dan, or all of us?" Lyra asked.

"I was meaning Mr. Best." He raised an eyebrow. "Unless you're planning on skipping town?"

This gave her the impression he was baiting her. "And why would I do that?"

"It's generally what people do when they have something to hide."

Lyra narrowed her gaze. "Not someone who has everything invested in her business. It sounds to me as though you are looking for a guilty person, which means you do suspect Rob was murdered."

For the first time, he seemed flustered. "You're deliberately twisting my words, and I don't have time for your amateur sleuthing."

He stormed out with his deputy, and Maggie followed to shut the door firmly behind them. "Wow. You sure tied him up in knots, Lyra. And talk about distrustful."

"He does seem very intrigued by you, dear." Patricia studied her thoughtfully. "As for Dan, I guess you're still a relative stranger to most people here." She grimaced. "I don't mean anything by that. I know you're innocent."

"It's okay. I guess I can see his point." Dan rubbed his face with both hands. "Only, I didn't ask him to leave me anything, and I don't know why Rob would do something so over the top that would upset his only son. No matter if they got on or not, I just can't picture Rob being insensitive in that way."

Lyra agreed and wondered why the sheriff couldn't see Dan was innocent. The annoying sheriff was on her mind a lot lately, and what did Mom mean by her comment? Why would he be intrigued by her? And why did that idea make her cheeks warm when he'd always acted as though he didn't trust her? She shook her head at this unaccustomed silliness and refocused on her friend. "Do you even want to own a garage, Dan? And did Rob ever ask if you might be interested?"

Dan stared out the window for a moment. "I know my way around an engine, but Rob was incredible. He understood just from the sound what was wrong and taught me how to listen for different things. The first time he showed me around the garage, I recall saying that it was a cool setup. I was also blown away when he let me help him work on the fun car he was doing up for himself and told him so." He turned back to her; the worry in his eyes intensified. "Do you think that's why he left it to me?"

Lyra smiled at Dan's inability to recognize his own worth

to another person. "He loved that garage more than anything. Maybe he wanted to leave it to someone who would feel the same way he did and keep it going rather than leaving it to his son who might not have any mechanical ability or interest."

"I guess that makes sense." He frowned again. "But I work for you, and besides, I don't have any business experience."

"Experience is something you gain over time," Maggie interjected. "What about when this house is finished? Are you going to move on, or will you wait tables and learn to cook?"

"I-I—" Dan hung his head. "We've always gone along on a day-to-day basis, and it never occurred to me it would end."

Lyra gave Maggie a pointed look. "Don't fret about it. It's not something I've given any thought to either. Whatever you decide to do, no one will talk you out of it. There will always be maintenance to do if you choose to stay with us." She meant it to sound positive, but even Mom grimaced. A man like Dan wanted to feel worthwhile, not to have tidbits given to keep him around.

"A garage sounds the perfect thing for a talented man like you." Patricia patted his shoulder. "I think if Rob wanted you to have it, for whatever reason, you should really give it some serious thought. Even if his son contests things."

"I don't know. It feels wrong to take something that should never be mine in the first place. If Rob was so unwell, he might have done this on a whim. Maybe he used it as a way to get his son to come to Fairview but didn't intend to keep the changes."

Lyra shook her head. "Listen to Mom and don't dismiss it straight away. See what the lawyer says before you rush into anything."

Dan scrapped his fingers through his hair. "I guess it

couldn't hurt to hear all sides of the story. I just wish Rob had mentioned it. That way I'd know exactly why he wanted me to have it, or if it was an impulse that he might have regretted but didn't have time to change. Would you mind coming with me, Lyra? You'll understand the legalese better than me."

"Hmm. You do know I lost a business?" she mused. "Maybe we should ask Maggie too. She's great at pulling things apart and getting to the point."

"Would you mind me being there?" Maggie asked.

He gave a weak smile. "The more the merrier. I've never been near a lawyer for myself, and I have to say it's a daunting prospect."

"You'll be fine. It's all about Rob, so there's nothing to fear," Lyra replied in what she hoped was an encouraging way. The truth was, she had a feeling that Rob's son wasn't going to make any of this easy, no matter what his father's intentions were. "You better check the mailbox in case Karl sent you a letter already."

"Why wouldn't he just ring or drop by?"

Lyra shrugged. "I'm not sure how things work in Fairview, but usually there's a letter."

Dan sighed resignedly. "I'll go check now."

They watched him wander down the driveway as if the weight of the world sat on his shoulders and he wasn't keen to get the letter.

Patricia tutted. "Poor boy is tied up in knots over this."

"Is it any wonder if he's being accused of taking advantage of Rob? As far as I'm concerned, Dan might not have known him for long, but they hit it off from day one and thought a lot of each other. Dan never had a dad, and I think Rob filled that gap nicely."

"Goodness. I never knew that about Dan." Patricia shook

her head. "Men have a bad habit of keeping things close to their chests."

They stared at each other. Lyra guessed that they were both thinking of particular men in their lives—the good and the bad. And Rob. What he'd done was so kind with regards to Dan, but what about his son? She agreed with Mom that Phillip had every right to be mad about part of his inheritance going to an almost stranger, but he'd assumed a great deal and it didn't seem that he was interested in having a discussion around trying to work it out. Surely, taking the claim to court was a last option and not where a rational person started from.

Plus, Dan didn't deserve to have his genuine feelings for Rob turned into something ugly. Was it possible to sort this out between them by using an intermediary? Dan would likely jump at the chance. Phillip, on the other hand, didn't appear to be amenable to other people's ideas or interference. Lyra wasn't sure if a mediator was possible in these situations, but she felt the question should at least be asked.

Dan arrived back and shook his head. "No letters."

"I wouldn't worry," Lyra reassured him. "I'm sure a lawyer deals with this kind of thing regularly. Karl will have a copy that you can look at, and he may very well have more answers."

He rubbed his head. "I can't believe that Rob is gone and that this is happening. It makes me sick to my stomach that we can't just mourn him and forget about who gets what."

"I know. We all want that. All you can do is take one step at a time, and the worst thing that could happen is that you don't get the garage."

Dan tilted his head. "It just occurred to me—would Phillip run the garage or sell it?"

"Good question. Would that make a difference to you?"

"A big difference. I don't have the money to buy it outright, but I might be able to get a loan."

"Hold that thought until you've spoken to the lawyer," Lyra smiled. "But it is great to have a plan."

In fact, she had just decided on a course of action that could go either way, but she owed it to Dan and Rob to get this sorted as soon as possible.

10

The others tried to talk her out of it, but Lyra was determined to have it out with Phillip. It was by no means a rash decision.

Taking an hour, she checked out Phillip McKenna on social media. He had no accounts. Was this to keep his father from knowing anything about him? Or did he have something to hide?

While searching his name, she found a small company in the town where Mom said he lived. Clicking on the link pulled up a page with a banner for a computing company specializing in fixing computers and setting up new ones for those who couldn't grasp the technology. It didn't mention his name, only the company name and phone number.

The facelessness of it was telling. Yet, it was also an occupation that helped people and would involve a great deal of person-to-person interaction, going back and forth to find out the needs and requirements of a customer. This gave her hope that she might be able to appeal to Phillip's better nature. Until she remembered—these days the process could be done online.

Squaring her shoulders, she stopped that train of thought in its tracks, and marched over to Rob's house. Knocking on the front door, she hoped Phillip was home so her courage wasn't wasted. After a while the door opened slightly, and he stared at her through the gap.

"I apologize for intruding, Mr. McKenna, and appreciate that me and my friends aren't your favorite people right now."

He glared. "You got that right. Is this going to take long?"

She took a steadying breath, reminding herself that the man was in mourning. It wasn't easy. "I'm here to ask if my bakery can provide the food for after the funeral."

His mouth fell open then snapped shut. "You're actually here to get business?"

"What?" Lyra gasped. "I'd never do that! I'm offering to supply the food and venue for free. We loved your father and are grieving along with most of the town. Getting together helps everyone through this loss, but it is a lot to deal with on your own and I'd like to help."

Phillip crossed his arms. "I'm not interested in a party. There will be a small funeral on Saturday morning if the police are done with their inquiries, and that's it."

"It wouldn't be a party. People gathering to pay their respects and to celebrate your father's life is usual. I'd really love to do this for him."

His nostrils flared. "I'm not interested in any gathering, and since my father just died under suspicious circumstances, I'd say leaving me alone would be top of the list of things you should do. In fact, I'd appreciate it being the only thing on the list."

The knot in her stomach tightened. Suspicious circumstances meant the police were still looking for clues to another person being involved. Did Phillip dislike his father enough to hurt him? But he couldn't be involved since he wasn't in town until after Rob's death. Which meant someone else was walking around town who knew something, even if they didn't actually kill him. She fought for a calm façade. "Just to be clear, you're not having anything after the funeral?"

"Finally, you understand. No, there will be nothing after the funeral, and this town won't bully me into it."

The self-satisfied smirk made her hands clench. "That was never the intention. I'll leave you to your grief, Mr. McKenna."

"Good. And don't think your offer of help will sway me from ensuring your friend doesn't steal my father's business."

The look he gave her was ugly, and as she went down the few steps, the door slammed behind. She flinched. Phillip McKenna was one angry man. It seemed that all he wanted to do was hurt someone, and that someone was gone. Clearly, this meant that the town, and especially Dan, would have to bear the brunt of it.

Inside the farmhouse, the others anxiously awaited the outcome. Lyra shook her head. "He's not interested in having anything after the funeral."

"That's not right," Dan growled.

"Sometimes people have good reasons not to." Patricia wiped her eyes with a tissue. "Only, Rob deserves a decent send-off, and I know he'd love for the town to get together and talk about having him in our lives. I feel so sad that I never got to say goodbye to him."

"Plenty of others feel the same." Lyra put an arm around her shoulders. "It isn't right, but what can we do?"

Dan paced the kitchen like a bear, and Maggie sat at the table, her chin resting on her palms, a picture of misery. The people in this house were just a few of the many who were fond of Rob, and Lyra knew she simply couldn't let this go.

"The funeral is on Saturday. The diner is always open on Saturdays."

They looked at her as if she were talking gibberish, and she smiled.

"Once I find out the actual time, we can invite everyone to come to the diner after the funeral. Instead of serving meals, we'll make it a wake of sorts. We'll supply tea and coffee and finger food for everyone who joins us."

Patricia leaned in to kiss her cheek. "What a lovely idea."

"It's a good size, but how will you get everyone in the diner?" Maggie asked, already in planning mode.

Lyra visualized the spaces. "It will be tight, but if we stack most of the tables out the back and hire extra chairs to place around the room, then we can have a few long tables inside for the food. Some people will have to stand, but most will move around while they chat anyway."

"There will definitely be some mixing and mingling, but extra chairs will be good for the elderly or infirm," Patricia agreed.

"Let's do it!" Dan grinned. "I'll handle the heavy lifting."

Maggie snapped her fingers. "I'll find out if we can borrow chairs from the community center."

"I'll bake some cakes and cookies right here."

"Good idea, Mom. I'll help Leroy make the hot food and get Poppy onto sandwiches."

"Will there be cupcakes?" Maggie's eyes twinkled. "Asking for a friend."

"Of course. Tell your friend there might even be a couple of flavors."

Cinnamon barked.

Maggie laughed. "She says thanks."

The mood was considerably lighter now that they were doing something positive instead of moping.

"We need to get the word out. Two days is not long," Lyra mused.

"Since I'm going to the community center, I can ask about the chairs and put up a flyer at the same time," Maggie offered.

Dan frowned. "Where do we get flyers from at such short notice?"

Maggie snorted. "We make them."

"I can fix almost anything, but I have no idea about craft type things."

"Then I guess it's me." Maggie gave an exaggerated sigh.

"You're very clever with that kind of thing, so I'm sure they'll be great."

"A compliment? Don't go all soft on me now, Danny boy."

He attempted a growl, but his eyes crinkled at the corners. "Wouldn't dream of it."

Patricia watched Maggie and Dan with a thoughtful expression, and Lyra hid a smirk. They were developing an interesting relationship and were oblivious to the fact that others could see it.

"I better go help Leroy and Poppy and let them know about Saturday. They were fond of Rob too, so I don't think they'll have any objections to helping out with this."

Leroy fumed as he flipped burgers. "How can he refuse to host his father's funeral?"

"It's just mean." Poppy's mouth quivered, and Cinnamon whined from the doorway, protective of her new friend.

"There's no point in getting upset about it," Lyra urged. "Phillip McKenna didn't know his father well, and maybe he has a business he needs to get back to in a hurry."

"Don't make excuses for the man." Leroy smashed his

spatula down on a burger pattie. "He's been in town five minutes and upset everyone he met. People want to give their condolences. How can he possibly take offense at that?"

"I don't know what his real problem is," Lyra admitted. "What I do know is that if we can do this for Rob, then I don't care if Phillip disapproves. This is my diner, and I choose what I do in it."

Leroy clapped his hands slowly. "Tell me what you need from us."

Lyra outlined the rough plan regarding the tables and chairs. "If we're expecting the mourners to eat from their laps, then we better make it all finger food. Cakes and cookies are taken care of. Could you make something hot?"

"Pigs in a blanket and mini meat pies—that the sort of thing?"

"They sound perfect." Lyra had an itch to make something fancier, but there wasn't time, and this was the kind of food the residents of Fairview knew and accepted as standard. "Mini quiche too?"

He nodded. "I'm all over that."

She smiled warmly. "I never had a doubt. I'll help, and Maggie will dress up a few tables to put the food on. Poppy, can you make sandwiches?"

"No problem. Earl will pitch in, won't you?"

He nodded enthusiastically. "If you show me how."

"Anything else?" Leroy asked.

"We need to spread the word. Maggie's making flyers right now, but we should tell everyone who comes in over the next two days and ask them to spread the word to as many people as possible."

He raised an eyebrow. "You do realize this will spread like wildfire? How do we cope with most of the town packed in here?"

"We'll use the back verandah too. A lot will have to stand,

but as I discussed with Mom earlier, that's what usually happens at a funeral anyway, right?"

Leroy nodded. "Rob will love this."

She smiled at the idea of Rob looking down on them and giving a thumbs up. "I think so."

"The knitting club's here today. Do you want to start there?" Poppy asked.

"That's perfect. If anyone can spread this faster, it's those lovely ladies."

"You got that right." Poppy laughed without taking offense, even though her mom was the leader of the group.

It was something Lyra often forgot, and she gave herself a mental memo to think before teasing about the group again. Slipping on her apron, she headed into the diner. The group were at their usual table and chatting like a flock of seagulls. Lyra was never sure if they heard what each other said, but they all showed up as regular as clockwork, so they must enjoy the dynamic.

"Hello, ladies. How are you?"

"We're very sad about Rob," Vanessa said glumly, and the others nodded.

"We all are," Lyra agreed, "but I'd like to suggest something to make us all feel slightly better."

Carrie-Ann Smith sniffed. "What could possibly do that?"

"A wake. Right here, straight after the funeral on Saturday."

"What do mean?" Martha frowned. "Is this instead of the one at the funeral home?"

"Not instead." Lyra enlightened them, "I'm sorry to say that there isn't going to be one at the funeral home."

Vanessa gasped. "That can't be right. Are you sure you're not trying to get more customers or something?"

Why it always came down to this, Lyra wasn't sure, but it annoyed the stuffing out of her. "Actually, Rob's son doesn't want to hold one, so I decided that I would. There is no charge, and all the food is free. It will be a gathering of his friends to say a proper goodbye."

"Well, now. That's different. Why didn't you say so?" Vanessa nodded as if giving her approval. "Shame on the boy, but good for you. We'll be here."

"I'm so glad. Would you be so kind as to spread the word?"

"That's the first time Vanessa's been asked to do what comes as natural as breathing," Carrie-Ann snickered.

This sent the other women off into peals of laughter. All except Vanessa, who looked down her nose at them until they stopped.

This was the first time since she'd heard about Rob that Lyra felt like laughing. Vanessa was indeed the biggest gossip of them all, but she was being supportive. Eventually. "Can I get you anything else today, ladies?"

"I think we're about done. Sitting here with these fools puts a person's teeth on edge after a while," Vanessa stated as she marched out the door.

When they were sure she really was gone, the other women let rip.

"Did you see her face?" Carrie-Ann giggled.

Martha held her stomach. "Oh my, I thought I would burst."

"You are so going to pay for that," June warned.

"It was worth it." Carrie-Ann brushed her hands against each other. "Now, Lyra, can we help out in any way?"

"That's sweet of you to offer, but we have it all under control."

"Then we'll help with the cleaning up and the dishes," Carrie Ann stated. "If we all do a little, it will take the pressure off."

Lyra didn't like to say that the dishwasher took care of

most things. If Carrie-Ann and the group wanted to help, then that was just fine with her. "We'd appreciate that."

"I'd like to be in charge of the flowers." Esther folded her knitting. "I do it for the church, and though I don't like to brag, they are always a talking point."

"That's wonderful! We hadn't gotten around to flowers yet."

Esther preened. "Flowers brighten every day, even those that are sad."

Not to be outdone, June's eyes lit up. "I have a beautiful photo frame I made. We could put it on a little table with a picture of Rob looking over the proceedings. I'll also bring my best lace cloth to place underneath."

The women nodded at each other, and Lyra's heart sighed at their generosity. This was why she'd left LA. People truly cared in Fairview. Mostly.

11

That night Lyra sat at the dining table, working on recipes for her next book, when Cinnamon ran to the front door and growled. A loud rap on the door sounded almost simultaneously. As soon as Lyra opened it, Phillip McKenna rounded on her.

"How dare you!"

Her heart pounded, but she stood her ground. This was clearly no social visit. "Excuse me?"

"You know exactly what I'm talking about. The party you're organizing at your diner after the funeral. I forbid it!"

Cinnamon was still growling, and now her top lip drew back.

"Please, stop shouting. You're upsetting my dog." Lyra motioned with her hand, and Cinnamon moved behind her; the growl continued, but was now more of a rumble.

"I don't give a fig newton about your stupid mutt. The darn thing wanders anywhere it chooses, sniffing around my kitchen and scratching at the doors."

Lyra stiffened. She could handle a little abuse but not

when it was directed at her girl. "Your father loved Cinnamon, and I daresay he used to feed her. She probably thinks you'll carry on in the same way. If she's being a nuisance, I'm sorry, but it may take her a while to appreciate Rob is gone—just like the rest of us."

Phillip paled. "You should tie her up until she does."

Lyra wasn't about to tie Cinnamon up and take away the freedom she loved, but offered what she thought was a good compromise. "No one else has any complaints about how friendly she is; however, I will try to keep her closer to home while you're in town."

"They're hardly likely to complain to the famous chef who can do whatever she likes because she has the town in the palm of her hand."

Lyra flinched as if he'd slapped her. "I don't know where you get your information, but you're misguided. In Fairview, I'm simply the diner owner."

He snorted. "Who sticks her nose into other people's business. I told you no party, and you went behind my back like the devious woman you are."

Lyra's hands locked on her hips. "There is no conspiracy here. I was completely open as you can see by the flyers out everywhere, and the townsfolk spread the word because they want this."

"You are the one instigating it against my direct orders."

Lyra felt her eyes bug. "Your orders? These days, I don't take orders from anyone. The last man who spoke to me this way is in jail." She hadn't meant to bring up her ex-agent and took a deep breath, which gave him an inroad.

"I heard everything about you being taken advantage of. Sounds unlikely to me when the rumors say that you couldn't handle the pressure and are hiding out in this one-horse town."

He was pushing all her buttons, but she held on to her temper. "You must choose to believe what you will, and we should get back to the real topic. While I am sorry for your loss, Mr. McKenna, I would argue that your father's friends have a right to mourn him as they see fit."

"The police might think otherwise."

Rather than being shocked, this frustrated her. "You'd really go that far to stop a farewell for your father?"

Phillip took a step closer. "I'd go much further to stop your interference in a private matter."

"Threats have no place here, Mr. McKenna." Dan loomed behind Phillip, who flinched. "I'll ask you to leave now, or I'll call the police for trespassing and save you the bother of having to call them yourself with such petty mindedness."

Dan moved back so Phillip could get by, which he did rather quickly. The look he gave her before he went down the steps chilled her to the bone.

"He is beyond furious. I hope he doesn't do anything silly," she told Dan.

Having arrived with Dan, Maggie stood to the other side of the doorway. "I don't trust him," she said as she came inside.

Dan gave Lyra a worried look. "Maybe you should think twice about the wake."

She shook her head. "I'm a big girl, and I won't be dictated to. All those years I was under Simon's thumb taught me to stand up for myself if I don't want to repeat my mistakes."

Dan nodded in the direction of Rob's house. "Normally I'd say you should stick to your guns, but that guy has such a huge grudge against his father he can't think straight. I'm worried about what he's capable of."

Maggie nodded. "He does seem determined to go against

every wish of his father's. Which means he'll want to ensure there is no farewell at the diner. At least until it's done, you should stay away from him."

"I don't mean to brush over your concerns, but the police are just down the road if he does try to ruin things. And with so many people around, what could he possibly do and manage to get away with?"

Even as Lyra posed the question, she thought about the men who'd tried to ruin her career before she moved here. From those experiences she knew there were some in this world who couldn't let a thing slide if they thought they could make things go their way. She didn't know Phillip well enough to say one way or the other if he fitted into this category, but he sure was mad enough to spoil things as he threatened to.

"I can see you won't be moved on this, but Maggie and I want you to take care not to be alone with him."

"I promise, Dan."

That went some way to appeasing him, but old habits die hard. Even though he'd been hired mainly as her driver, Dan had been looking out for her for a few years. She didn't want him to get in trouble by defending her—should the need arise.

Which she certainly wasn't discounting.

Her phone rang just then, and her heart lifted when she saw the number. It was Kaden, and he wanted to make it a video call. She hadn't been prepared for that and hoped she didn't look a mess. Excusing herself, she accepted the invite on the way to her bedroom. His smile beamed out from her mobile screen.

"Hello, gorgeous!"

"Hardly." She laughed. "How are you doing?"

"Great. Business hasn't slacked since the reopening after

the fire, but I won't let that stop me from getting over there soon."

"I'm looking forward to it." Shutting the bedroom door that she currently shared with Maggie, Lyra sat in the large comfy chair by the window which overlooked the stream. "Although, you might want to leave it for a while longer."

"Uh-oh. That doesn't sound good." He leaned into the screen. "What's happened?"

She sighed. "I don't like to bring you down, but there's been a death, and it looks suspicious."

"What?" His eyebrows hit his hairline. "Define suspicious."

"That's just it—I don't know. No one's said that it is murder, but the police are asking questions that point that way." Lyra sucked in a big breath. "Rob was a friend of the family, and we're all very upset about his death, and so is most of the town."

"Sorry, my tact seems to have left the building with the shock of it."

She waved his apology away. "I'm sure you're thinking that this can't be happening again. I can't lie. That was my reaction once I accepted Rob was dead and then realized it might not have been by natural causes."

"If that's the case, do the police think you're involved in some way?" he asked gently.

"Initially, I think they might have. Right now, it's actually Dan who's on their radar."

"Dan," he scoffed. "That's nuts."

"Of course, it is. Dan thought the world of Rob."

Kaden frowned. "Is this the guy Dan was living with?"

She'd forgotten how much Kaden knew about her life in Fairview, which naturally included Dan, Maggie, and Mom. "That's right. They became good friends, which upset Rob's son, who thinks Dan wheedled his way into his father's will."

"Ahh. Now it makes sense why they're looking in his direction."

"That's only because they don't know him well. There's no proof Dan did anything wrong, and there are no clues as to who might have."

"We both know how frustrating that is. It took weeks for them to figure out who started the fire in my restaurant. How are you holding up?"

She smiled. "Just talking to you and saying this stuff aloud helps. Rob's son is rude and aggressive, and it doesn't matter how pleasant I am, the chip on his shoulder is as big as Mt. Rushmore."

Kaden sucked in a deep breath. "Maybe I should get down there."

"No, please, don't do that. You're busy, and I'm simply venting. Besides, Mom's home now, and I have Maggie. Plus Dan's moved back into the house."

"That's all fine, but knowing how your mind works, there's no way you'll sit back and let the police handle things."

She reddened. "I don't know what you mean."

"Don't give me that innocent look," he scoffed. "Why not let the police deal with this and be a little patient?"

Patience was fine, but not unlimited. Worry laced his words, and she changed her mind about telling him her theory. "I'm so glad you rang and talked some sense into me."

"Did I?" he asked doubtfully.

"Of course. Now I really should get back to my book-work, and I'm sure you've got better things to do."

He shook his head. "Never think you're not important to me. Promise you'll call if you need anything."

"I promise, and thanks for listening."

When the screen went blank, Lyra cradled the phone to

her chest. It would be so good to have him here, and he'd come if she asked, but she couldn't put him through another convoluted case. It was bad enough Dan was involved, and that Maggie and Mom had to be around this drama.

As well as Leroy, Poppy, and Earl.

12

"Goodness, this looks official. What did you do now?" Carrie-Ann asked a little too gleefully.

Lyra was at the counter when the sheriff came in with two deputies a little after opening. "I'm sure we'll find out soon enough. Take a seat and I'll get your order packed up in a jiffy."

Disappointed, the woman did sit—as close to the counter as possible.

Sheriff Walker raised an eyebrow before motioning to Lyra. "Ms. St. Claire, could we have a word with you out back?"

Lyra led them into the kitchen, then wondered if Carrie-Ann would get a crick in her neck if she leaned anymore to watch through the gap. "Poppy, can you box up an order please," she called across the room.

Poppy's eyes bugged at the police. "Sure."

When she'd hurried out, Lyra turned to the men. "What can I do for you?"

The sheriff nodded at Leroy over at the grill before he spoke. "We have the autopsy report."

Something in his eyes made her skin tingle. Whatever he had to say wasn't going to be good, and he was clearly watching for her reaction to it. She clasped her hands over her apron and waited.

"The doctor who examined Mr. McKenna thought he'd had a heart attack."

Lyra's stomach flipped. "Are you saying he didn't?"

"After checking Mr. McKenna's records, it was discovered that although there was a history of high blood pressure, he was on medication, but otherwise healthy and fit for a man his age."

Leroy turned off the grill and came forward, wiping his hands on a towel. "I could have told you that and saved some time. What exactly are you trying to say, and why all this beating around the bush?"

The sheriff frowned but kept his eyes on Lyra. "The coroner did a toxicology, and it appears that something he ingested may have led to his heart failure."

Her eyes narrowed. She'd been accused of murder before. It wasn't something you got used to. "Are you suggesting again that I was the one to give him whatever it was he ate?"

"We believe he dined here most days, and…"

"That's right." She cut him off. "He ate whatever I was cooking along with much of the town. There hasn't been one upset stomach that I'm aware of, or anything else you could lay at my door."

Walker's nostrils flared. "What I was about to ask was, the rest of his meals were eaten at his residence with Mr. Best, weren't they?"

Lyra gasped, suddenly seeing where this was going. "Rob could have eaten anything anywhere other than those two places."

"I don't imagine that's likely, given the time constraints of his working days."

"Look, I don't like what you're inferring. What I do know is that Dan would never harm Rob. Why are you assuming he could be the only culprit?"

Sheriff Walker stiffened. "I don't know what would give you that impression. I'm merely doing my job."

"When is hounding a man doing your job?"

Spots of color suffused his cheeks. "When everything points to having not only access, but a motive."

"There has to be other persons of interest. Wait a minute. Did Rob's son put you up to this, because of the garage?"

"I can assure you that my department doesn't rely on members of the public for all its evidence. We ascertain what facts are pertinent to the case."

"Then I suggest you get back out there and find more facts and stay clear of the fiction that you seem to be so keen on."

"There is no need to be rude, Ms. St. Claire," he growled.

"Isn't there? You come in here and scare everyone, then calmly slander my friend. How did you think I would react?"

"In a civil manner. Clearly, I expected too much as usual. The death is being treated as suspicious, and therefore we are asking people to help us with our inquiries. Now, where can I find Mr. Best today?"

"He's at my house. Working as usual." Lyra didn't do sullen, but that's how it came out as she fought to keep her anger in control. Anger that Rob had been poisoned and horror that someone would potentially let Dan take the blame.

Leroy came to her once they'd gone and put a hand on her shoulder. "Pay him no mind. He hates it when a case eludes him, and no matter how it seems, he's a good cop and he was fond of Rob."

"I never would have guessed it by the way he acts." Her

voice shook, and she squeezed her hands together to stop them from shaking.

"It's all for show. Coming up through the ranks in a small town is hard. Not everyone can get past him arriving in town as a wet-behind-the-ears kid straight out of the academy. He wants to prove that he's got what it takes to do the job."

"That might be true, but it's no reason to focus all his attention on Dan."

"I think he was here to see what you thought of the whole thing. You know, get your opinion." He snorted. "He really could have phrased it better."

The idea shocked her into silence for several seconds. "I don't understand why you think he'd want my opinion."

"Maybe to give him an idea if he was headed in the right direction, or if there was any validity in Phillip McKenna's allegations. I believe he holds you in pretty high esteem."

"I find that hard to believe." She dismissed what she could only think of as a fanciful notion. "So, you think that Phillip was the one who suggested Dan was the—I can't even say it."

"The murderer?" Leroy filled in the blank.

She nodded.

"To me it seems the most likely. Like you said, he's not happy that Dan will inherit something that belongs to the estate of a man he barely knew."

"You could say the same of Phillip. To all accounts, he was the one who decided not to have any contact with his father. Why would he think he had the only claim on everything his father owned?"

Leroy gave her a pensive look. "Because that's how it's always been—around here and most small towns. Businesses and property stay in the family unless they lose them. End of story."

As much as she hated to admit it, Leroy made perfect sense.

"I understand all that, and if circumstances were different I'd encourage Dan to walk away, but I believe Rob knew what he was doing and that he wanted the garage to go to someone who would take care of it in the same way he did. That would have mattered more to him than money or whatever else he owned."

"You won't get any arguments from me about his reasons."

Something about the way Leroy said it made her ask, "Do you think I should butt out?"

"Now don't put words in my mouth," he blustered.

"It's all over your face."

Leroy smiled gently. "Inciting the police and Phillip McKenna won't help anyone, least of all Dan. You've got the lawyer to see, and you'll need to be calm and reasonable at that appointment to help Dan decide what to do."

Lyra knew he was right. Although it did rankle for a few minutes that Leroy implied she wasn't being reasonable. Then again, since the day Rob introduced them and Leroy told her that he didn't cook anything fancy, she'd always admired his honesty. Since she encouraged it, how could she fault him for speaking his mind? "Okay. For Dan's sake, I'll do my best even if Phillip provokes me."

"Good for you."

"Can I just ask what kind of medication Rob was on?"

Leroy shook his head. "Beta blockers. Now, I can hear things are picking up out there. The breakfast rush must be in."

On cue, orders began to print off near the grill, and the register sounded as if it were singing. Earl hurried by with a tray full of dirty dishes, which he deposited on the counter, and grabbed an empty one without pause. Lyra would have to wait until after the rush to talk to Dan and find out how the sheriff's visit went.

And she would definitely look up how beta blockers worked.

Dan was gone a long time, and Lyra worried that he'd been taken into custody as there was no sign of the police either. She glanced out across the veranda many times and even wandered down the path once or twice, to no avail. On each occasion, Cinnamon came to greet her, and not for the first time, she wished the beagle could talk. No one cared what they said around a dog, and she would bet Cinnamon had spent some time at Dan's side during the interrogation. Or interview.

Finally, he appeared at the window on the veranda and crooked a finger. She wiped her hands on her apron with dread and went outside. "You don't look good. What's wrong?"

"Don't worry, the police just asked the usual questions like where I was and who I was with. I'm sure I have as much or as little of an alibi as half the town."

"If their visit went okay, why do you look so upset?"

"Karl Lowe stopped by just as the police left and made it official. We have a meeting Monday morning to go over the will."

"And that bothers you?"

"For all the reasons I've spoken about. Plus, I've never dealt with this kind of thing before. My parents are both alive, and no one else ever wanted to leave me a thing."

Lyra had to ask, "Did Karl tell you what the will says?"

Dan raked his fingers through his short hair. "He wouldn't go into details but did admit that the garage was bequeathed to me. With stipulations."

She put a hand on his arm. "If he didn't explain the stipulations, then you know as much as you possibly can today. Try not to worry. All you have to do is go to the meeting to find out the rest, right?"

"But Phillip McKenna will be there."

"Dan, you've dealt with worse things. You went to war for goodness' sake."

"That's different. I understood what was expected and could envisage different scenarios, so I knew how to plan and react in each case."

"Maybe, but Phillip's only weapons are words. What is the worst that can happen? He might yell a bit and argue, but it won't affect the outcome."

He suddenly gave a wry grin. "When you put it like that, I guess I am being a wimp."

"Not at all. I get that this is a big deal for you, but it's not the biggest thing you've ever had to face, right?"

He nodded. "Thanks for the pep talk, Boss."

"No charge."

He was smiling, but she knew it still bothered him. Poor Dan. He was a black-and-white kind of guy and taking something he hadn't exactly earned was hard for him to accept.

13

L ater that morning, they discovered Phillip's next move. Vanessa came bearing the local paper, which Lyra hadn't had a chance to look at. She slammed it on the counter to show the note about Rob's death, advising that the funeral was a private affair to be held at lunchtime that very day. This could only have come from Phillip, and the town was not happy. At least every person who came in the diner complained loudly about it.

When Poppy's mom clapped her hands to draw everyone's attention, the young woman slunk out to the kitchen, and Lyra had a strong urge to follow her.

"This is unacceptable!" Vanessa stood at her usual table, surrounded by the knitting ladies, and spoke loudly over the din. "The church service should be for everyone. Someone should speak to Rob's son and tell him that."

"You do it, Vanessa. Everyone listens to you," Carrie-Ann urged.

The others nodded effusively. Vanessa's eyes widened, then she snatched up her bag and marched out the door to the cheers of her team, who remained behind with their lattes.

Remembering Leroy's suggestion to not involve herself further, Lyra kept her silence, but when Vanessa came back ten minutes later, red-faced, and more out of sorts than before, raging about going to the police, she had to say something.

"I'm not sure that would be wise or even worthwhile. If Mr. McKenna wants a private service, then he is within his rights, and the police won't be able to stop him from doing so."

"I'll thank you not to give me any advice. You don't know our ways, and that odious man has left me with no choice. He can't come swanning in here and tell us we have no right to say goodbye to our dear friend. He ignored his father all this time, so why should he get to dictate everything? It isn't right or charitable." Vanessa sniffed, her chin wobbling, and marched back out again.

The new round of cheers was short-lived when ten minutes later, Vanessa returned, despondent. "The sheriff says his hands are tied."

"At least you tried." Lyra fetched fresh coffee, not wanting to point out to the distressed woman that she recently said as much. The news must have filtered through, because a minute or two later, Poppy came to check on her mom.

Even knowing this would be the outcome of Vanessa's visit, Lyra felt it was rather sweet that the woman had made the effort. This new side of her character softened the impression that she was merely the town meddler. Instead, it showed that she did care about others.

"Maybe we can't get to the church or the funeral home, but we can say all our goodbyes tonight in a way that Rob would love—with all his friends together in one place."

Vanessa dabbed her eyes. "I don't see that we have a

choice. Thank you, Lyra. Poppy, I saw a lovely black shawl in the store window down the street. Would you mind picking it up for me?"

Poppy was also tearful, but she hugged her mom and nodded. "Of course, if it's still open."

Lyra smiled, enjoying the display of love. "Go now, just in case."

With a grateful look, Poppy hurried to get her bag and raced out.

Vanessa grimaced. "She still has her apron on."

"Never mind. She'll be there and back before anyone notices."

The raised eyebrow was enough to get Lyra back into work mode.

The turnout at the diner was bigger than she could have imagined, and people stood in clusters inside and out on the veranda. It started very somberly and with a fair amount of talk about Phillip McKenna.

"He has no right to waltz in here and deprive us of saying goodbye," Vanessa informed anyone who would listen, which turned out to be many.

Before the ill feeling could take hold and turn the afternoon into something dark, Lyra made her way into the middle of the main group in the diner. "It would be lovely to visit the grave a little later, but for now why don't we talk about Rob and remember him the way he deserves."

Vanessa sniffed. "Rob was kind and wouldn't have wanted his son to treat us with such disrespect."

Esther Rand nodded. "He was a fine man. I should have married him when I had the chance."

"You?" Carrie-Ann gasped. "I think you'll find that Rob

set his cap at me several times. If I'd have said the word, his boots would be outside my door today."

"You're both talking nonsense," Vanessa announced. "Rob was a confirmed bachelor who liked to help anyone who needed a hand. He kindly carried my shopping home on a regular basis."

"He carried your shopping home because you ordered him to," Carrie-Ann muttered.

Lyra's shoulders shook as she went back to handing around plates and napkins. Rob had clearly stolen many hearts—whether he wanted to or not.

Mom placed a cherry pie on one of the tables and smiled wryly. "Rob was a sweetie, that's why he helped them all, but his love for his wife was enough to keep him out of their clutches."

"Shhh." Lyra glanced around. "Don't let them hear you."

"Hah! They can't hear a thing over their own voices."

Poppy came up behind her to whisper in Lyra's ear. "The police are here."

Sure enough, Sheriff Walker appeared at the door with Officer Moore at his side.

Lyra hurried to them, closely watched by everyone else. "Sheriff, are you here to pay your respects, or is there a problem?"

Walker removed his hat. "I'm afraid this is police business. I can see for myself that you're not serving alcohol today, but do you have a license for this many people?"

Lyra's stomach twisted. "I guess I should have thought about that, but it's a wake, and they're not paying customers."

"Nevertheless, the code won't cover even half this many people, so it's a fire hazard." He leaned in and lowered his voice. "I'm sorry. There was a complaint."

She sighed. "Let me guess, Rob's son put you up to this, didn't he?"

Walker stood back and returned to his usual staunchness. "I didn't make the rules, but I do have to implement them."

While she understood his position, with so many people wanting to say goodbye, Lyra wished he'd make an exception. Unaware of what was transpiring, inside the diner people were mostly laughing, as they regaled each other with tales. True or false, who could say, but from what she'd already heard, they were usually hilarious. "What a shame to send everyone away."

When she turned back to him, a movement by the back door drew her attention. Cinnamon ran down to the gap in the hedge then looked back at Lyra. Maybe she was reading more into the behavior, but the silent message was loud and clear in her mind. "What if there was a private party at my house?"

Walker's mouth felt open. "You'd invite this lot?"

"Why not? We've barely begun, and there is a ton of food. I have a huge backyard, and we can put all the chairs out there. If they're not all crowded into one room and it's a private party, I'm not breaking any codes, right?"

He nodded. "As long as the noise isn't too bad and it finishes at a decent time, the police would have no reason to interfere."

"Thank you, Sheriff." Lyra meant it sincerely. His tone and manner had changed significantly, and though she had no idea why, she wasn't about to question it.

He shuffled his feet, adding, "The town thanks you. This means a lot to all of us."

She raised an eyebrow, thinking of someone who might disagree with his statement, but let it go and was glad when he offered to help.

"Since I'm off duty as of now, I could carry some chairs. I'll see you tomorrow Officer Moore."

The woman hesitated looking as surprised by her boss's

attitude as Lyra was. It took a second or two after the woman had gone before Lyra to remember her manners. "That would be great. Could you give me a minute to tell them?" Without waiting for a reply, Lyra marched inside. "Ahem! Excuse me, everybody."

The voices didn't falter.

"Perhaps a bit of height might be a good idea." Walker lifted her onto the nearest chair.

Flustered at his manhandling, which she had to admit was done gently, Lyra couldn't speak for a second. Walker stuck two fingers in his mouth and whistled loud enough to bring in sheep from the next town. Then he casually nodded for her to continue. The surprises kept on coming, she mused.

"Due to circumstances out of my control, the wake has to be moved to my farmhouse. Please take your glass, and if you can manage your chair, that would be great. Follow me out through the veranda to my backyard, where we can continue celebrating Rob's life."

The noise rose again, filled with questions she pretended she couldn't hear. Dan and Maggie looked about ready to burst with curiosity as well, but they quickly got to work stacking chairs when the other mourners moved out of the way.

Like the pied piper, Lyra picked up a couple of platters and led them down the cobbled path to her front yard. They followed her down the side of the house to a flat area that overlooked the stream. Large weeping willows gave it a fairy-tale grotto effect, and Cinnamon ran ahead to stand at the perfect spot to set up the chairs and tables. Twenty minutes later Lyra was handing around platters and joining in the laughter.

Cinnamon nudged her hand, and she followed the caramel gaze. A lone figure stood on the other side of the stream; half hidden by the bows of large trees. Arabelle. In the waning light and across the distance, Lyra couldn't make out her face, but the body language could not be mistaken. Her head was bent, and several times her hands swiped at her eyes.

Lyra didn't know what to make of this. Arabelle hadn't been to the diner since Rob's death, and they hadn't had a great relationship from what Lyra saw. Yet, the woman was obviously upset. Was it because of Rob? If so, then why wouldn't she come to the wake if she felt that way? Perhaps she was embarrassed for people to see a softer side when she went out of her way to show that none existed. Lyra had a strong urge to go and personally invite Arabelle to join them, even though she must have heard about the wake and could see what was going on here across the water.

She had no more time to ponder this. Cinnamon nudged her hand again and whined, then ran back up the yard to the hedge. She looked back at Lyra, barked furiously, and disappeared between the gap. Something was very wrong.

Thrusting the platter at Vanessa, who was the closest, Lyra mumbled something about handing it around and ran towards the diner. She'd reached the hedge when a hand grabbed her arm and she squealed.

The sheriff stepped out of the shadows. "What's the rush?"

Heart pounding, Lyra shrugged his hand off her arm. "I'm on my way to find out. Come if you must, but hurry up and decide because Cinnamon is upset about something."

She ran through the gap, up the steps of the veranda, and across to the back door of the diner. It was wide open. Walker had followed, but now he pushed his way in front of her and entered first. It didn't occur to Lyra to be annoyed as she peered over his shoulder into the well-lit kitchen.

A body lay on the floor.

14

Leroy lay on his side; a trickle of blood ran from the back of his head and down his neck. And another cut on his forehead was also bleeding. The two gashes pooled beneath him. There was an awful lot of blood.

"He's been attacked," she said needlessly, not liking how still Leroy was and hoping the attacker was gone.

While Walker cautiously looked around the room, peering out into the diner and into the small hallway, Lyra knelt beside Leroy to feel for a pulse. "He's breathing—call the paramedics."

While he did so, Lyra grabbed two clean cloths and placed them over the wounds, applying pressure. Just then Dan and Maggie ran through the doorway and hurried to her side.

Walker had turned on the rest of the lights, and he called to them from the diner doorway. "Stay with Leroy, I'm going to check the restrooms."

Dan did what Lyra wanted to but couldn't, and followed Walker at a distance.

"Is he okay?" Maggie asked.

She nodded. "I think so. His pulse is still strong despite

the blood loss. It must have happened recently. Someone must have been watching the diner and waited until we'd all left."

"How do you know he didn't fall and whack his head on the way down?"

"There are two cuts. Look at the way he fell. His knees must have given way from the blow to the back of his head, and he fell forward. Maybe he hit his head on the floor. Yes, look, there's blood by the dishwasher."

Maggie stared as if unsure who she was. "You are scarily good at this, unless that's just a guess."

Lyra shrugged. "I guess I watch too much CSI."

Leroy groaned; his hand went straight to the back of his head.

She pulled his hand away. "Shhh! Steady, Leroy. You've got a couple of head wounds. Just relax, the paramedics are on their way. You need to lie still until they get here."

He groaned again but did as she asked. "Did you see them?"

"Them? There was more than one attacker?"

"I'm not sure." He squinted across the room. "Who's that?"

Voices from the diner came closer.

"It's only Dan and the sheriff," Lyra said soothingly. "They're looking for whoever did this."

"The place is empty," Walker informed them once he entered the room. He gave a tight smile when he saw that Leroy had come around. "Do you know who attacked you?"

Leroy shook his head and hissed out a breath, clutching his temple with his free hand. "The coward hit me from behind. I was scrubbing a pot and leaned under the sink to get another scraper. With the music playing, I didn't hear a thing until it was too late. Then I was falling. The floor rushed up to meet me and the lights went out."

"Well, at least you know it wasn't any of us," Dan stated flatly.

Lyra nodded. "We also know for sure that no one next door could have done it, but there is at least one person who wasn't there—"

"Hold on a minute," Walker interrupted. "It may seem like it, but not everyone in Fairview is over at your place."

Lyra was about to dispute that, when the paramedics arrived. She backed away to give them room and stood several feet back by the grill with Maggie. Now that Leroy was being attended to, her brain worked overtime running through suspects.

"I hate to say it, but the sheriff is right," Maggie spoke quietly. "There's a heap of people next door, but not everyone in town is there."

Lyra nodded again. "I was just thinking the same thing. Not only was Phillip and a few others not there, I saw Arabelle across the stream watching us. Of course, it's laughable that Arabelle would hurt Leroy."

"Especially when we know who had the biggest grudge around here," Maggie agreed.

"Arabelle? How long was she there?"

Lyra frowned at the sheriff, who was quiet on his feet for such a big man. "I have no idea, but I can't imagine she did this to Leroy and then sprinted down the road and around the corner to that side of the stream."

"Hmmm. It doesn't seem likely," he admitted.

Lyra was a little surprised that he agreed with her about anything these days, and it gave her the encouragement to continue. Which was probably never his intention. "Phillip McKenna might have a grudge against Dan, and me, but why Leroy? Phillip loves the way Leroy cooks his steak. If he didn't like him, he'd hardly eat here, would he?"

"The fact that he doesn't like you hasn't stopped him from

coming to the diner, so I don't know if not liking Leroy is enough to keep him away either."

Did the sheriff realise that he'd just admitted that Phillip had a strong motive?

"Good point. The trouble is, I don't know of anyone who disliked Leroy."

"Just like Rob," Maggie added.

"If you don't count his son, or Arabelle," Dan added.

"You're making my head spin," Leroy muttered and closed his eyes.

He was terribly pale. Probably due to the loss of blood.

"Don't worry, Leroy, the sheriff will find out who did this." Lyra thought this was the right thing to say, but with no suspect yet for Rob's murder, she wasn't instilled with a great deal of confidence.

Once Leroy was taken from the diner, Lyra, Maggie, and Dan headed outside. They looked over to the hedge where many guests spilled into the car park. While they might not know what was going on, the paramedic's siren would have alerted them to it being an injury, and there were bound to be plenty of questions.

"I guess the evening is done," Maggie said sadly.

"Just as Phillip McKenna wanted." Suddenly cold, Lyra hugged herself.

Walker shuffled his feet behind them. "Let's keep that talk to ourselves for now. If the crowd gets wind of his complaint to shut the wake down, they'll likely lynch him. Since we have no proof he hurt Leroy, I don't want to encourage any vigilante behavior."

"Proof?" Dan gasped. "You can't be serious."

"Deadly serious. I will be speaking to Mr. McKenna, but right now there is no proof he did anything to Leroy."

"Well, I'd love to hear his alibi," Dan growled again.

"That's not helping," Walker growled back.

Lyra frowned at him. "Since we can't be relied upon not to express our views, I think it best that you explain to the guests that we should probably call it a night. Then you can phrase it in your terms, and we don't have to lie."

"Very well." Without a backward glance, he led them down the path.

Lyra wasn't looking forward to the reactions from the crowd. Regardless of what Walker wanted, and how he phrased things, she had no doubt that a lot of people would jump to the same conclusion about Phillip McKenna. The small upside was that at least Walker would be on hand to field their questions.

As expected, they were barely at the hedge when the barrage began.

"What's going on at the diner?" Vanessa demanded.

Walker made a way through for himself and Lyra and moved into the middle of the largest group. When he put his hand up, the chatter slowly died down. "There's been an incident at the diner. Leroy's been attacked, and it would be for the best if everyone heads home."

"What do you mean, attacked?" Carrie-Ann clutched Vanessa's arm.

Vanessa shook her off. "That place seems to attract disaster. First Rob and now Leroy. Who will be next?"

The sheriff scowled at her. "Let's remain calm, Mrs. Fife. I'll ask you all to finish up now and give your details to the deputy at the gate. Your safety is more important than this gathering, so make sure you leave with at least one other person."

"Are you saying that someone's out there who could harm us?" Martha Curran squeaked.

"I'm merely asking everyone to take precautions until we find out who did this."

At that moment, two of his deputies jogged up the path,

and he hurried over to join them. Explaining the situation quickly, he sent one to the bottom of the driveway.

Lyra saw and heard the horror spread around the mourners and stepped forward. "I'm terribly sorry we have to cut this short. Please take a plate of food with you as you leave."

Oddly, that got them motivated.

Lyra found her mom who, though pale, was busy consoling Martha, a sobbing Poppy, and a few others. Cinnamon did the rounds, putting her paw up to people and allowing herself to be petted. She broke away from the group and came toward Lyra.

"Are you okay, Mom?"

"I was about to ask you the same thing."

"It was a terrible shock, but I'm hopeful that he'll be fine. Leroy has no family in town, so once we get everything cleaned up in the diner tomorrow, I'd like to go to the hospital and check on him. Will you help out at the diner, if I go after the breakfast rush?"

Mom didn't hesitate. "Of course. The poor man needs someone to care for him."

"I'll come with you," Maggie offered.

"I think it's best if I hang around here and watch both the farmhouse and the diner." Dan glanced around at the dwindling crowd. "The police will have their hands full questioning everyone."

He was right, and as they said goodbye to the last of the stragglers, Lyra noticed that most of the food was gone. It occurred to her that some might meet up in smaller groups elsewhere to discuss the day's happenings. If that were so, they not only would be safer, but her food wouldn't go to waste. After all his effort, Leroy would be pleased by that, and right now, she desperately needed something good to focus on.

They cleaned up the yard, and Dan loaded up large plastic baskets with the dirty crockery and glasses.

"These are heavy. Why don't you carry the platters and leftover food back to the diner, and I'll bring these a few at a time?"

Lyra had already attempted to pick one up and had to gratefully agree. Stacking several large platters together, she led them through the hedge. "Lucky all the lights are still on in the diner."

From beside her, Poppy peered ahead up the path with Cinnamon nosing around them. "Are the police still there?"

"Looks that way, so we may not be allowed inside. If that's the case, we should leave everything on the veranda."

"What about the food?" Maggie asked. "Animals might get up here and make a mess."

"There's not much left. Everyone, take what you like home. We'll trash the rest."

Poppy shook her head. "Thanks, but I'm not hungry."

"Me either," Earl echoed.

"You might want something later, dear. Take a little bit just in case," Mom insisted.

Poppy nodded, her eyes glued to the police inside the kitchen. Walker beckoned to Lyra through the glass, and she went inside a couple of feet.

"Don't worry, I understand this is a crime scene. We plan to leave everything outside overnight."

"Perfect. I wanted you to know that we should be done soon, but just in case we need to come back in the morning, I'm going to put tape across all the external doors."

"This might sound crass, but will I be able to open tomorrow?"

"I should think so. It will depend on what we find, so I'll let you know first thing in the morning one way or the other."

She nodded. "I'd appreciate that."

"I will have to question your staff at some stage."

"I'm sure we're all expecting that. Would you mind grabbing me a couple of trash bags so I can bag up the leftover food? As Maggie pointed out, we don't want animals getting at it and making a mess. They're in the bottom drawer under the counter by the dishwasher."

He did as she asked, carefully stepping around the blood, and handed her the bags. "If you leave me a set of keys, I'll lock up so you don't have to hang around."

"Leroy's are hanging up by the coat rack." She pointed to her left. "I'll see you tomorrow then."

He nodded and headed back to the scene. Lyra gulped. That pool of blood would likely give her nightmares.

15

Sunday was a stunning spring morning, and Lyra was up early. It had been hard to sleep, and judging by the bleary faces that greeted her in the kitchen, the rest of the household had the same experience.

They didn't talk much until they left the house.

"I wonder how Leroy is," Dan said.

"I'll call the hospital when it's a reasonable hour."

"The lights are already on in the diner, or did you leave them on last night?"

Lyra quickened her stride. "I left the sheriff in charge of locking up."

To her relief, Walker was inside, and he came and opened the door.

"I was worried there was a break-in," she told him.

"It was too early to trouble you. I wanted to come back in before anyone arrived to have another look in case I missed something. This way you can open as soon as I take the tape down."

It was nice of him to think of her business, and Lyra

followed him inside while the others waited on the veranda. "You're here on your own?"

"All the hard work was done last night. This was an opportunity to think on it quietly and, as I said, do one last sweep."

She glanced around the kitchen, which had been left as it was from last night. With one major exception. "Did you clean up the blood?"

He shuffled his feet. "I had some time."

"That's very thoughtful of you, and I appreciate it."

Walker shrugged. "You shouldn't have to face that again."

They stood there awkwardly for a few moments until Dan coughed behind them.

"Could I bring in the dishes so we can start loading the dishwasher? Only, there are quite a few."

Walker slipped into sheriff mode. "I'll get rid of the tape and should be out of your way in a couple of minutes."

"What about talking to my staff?" Lyra reminded him.

"I have a few things to do first and should be back after the breakfast rush is over." He sighed. "You'll probably have your hands full again with well-wishers."

"More like rubberneckers," Maggie groaned.

After the last few days, Lyra felt exhausted just thinking about how her customers would hound her for answers when she knew no more than they did. "Thanks for understanding. Like Rob, people think a lot of Leroy, and without him in the kitchen, it will likely be frantic."

"I don't envy you. The tape I took from the back door is on the counter. I'll leave you to get rid of it if I may, and I'll go take care of the rest."

She put it in the bin, which needed emptying, but along with a lot of other things, it would have to wait. Dishes and getting the tables and chairs back to their proper positions took precedence. Tying her apron, she turned to her team, who were all inside by now. "We're all clear and good to open. Earl offered to come in today, even though it's his day off, but we need to get started on the cleaning and tidying up now, if you're all up for it?"

Dan placed a second load by the dishwasher. "Of course. I'll keep bringing through the dirty dishes and load them until Earl gets here. While I'm waiting for them to wash, I'll put everything back to where it should be in the diner."

"How about I sweep the floor in there first," Mom offered.

"And I'll load the cabinets with anything we have available from the refrigerator, so we have something for when the first customers show up." Maggie rolled her eyes. "I'm thinking there will be plenty of them again."

"The sheriff said as much. Thank goodness you're all here to get the diner back on track. I'm so grateful for your help."

They shrugged it off, but it was wonderful, as well as a relief, to know they were as determined as she was not to let what happened to Leroy derail the diner; Lyra had to push down the wave of emotion which threatened to overwhelm her. "I'll get some food underway and make coffee."

"I won't say no to that," Dan called on his way out the back door.

With so many hands, they managed a great deal in the hour before Poppy showed up, and Earl wasn't far behind her.

"Poppy, could you open up, please?"

With the diner back to how it was before the wake, and the dishwasher going non-stop, they were catching their collective breath with fresh coffee. Leroy had cleaned most of the kitchen before he was attacked, so Lyra already had a batch of muffins in the oven, made porridge, and now soup bubbled away on the stove. It wasn't much, but better than she'd hoped for.

Poppy slowly put on her apron, her eyes wide, as she

walked around the kitchen and stopped in front of the place where Leroy had lain.

"Are you okay, dear?" Mom asked.

The girl blinked several times. "Yes, sorry. I just can't get my head around Leroy being hurt."

"Yeah, whoever did it needs to go to jail for a very long time," Earl said harshly.

"It was despicable," Poppy's voice hitched. "I hope he's going to be okay."

Lyra put an arm around her shoulders. "I know it's not easy, but if we're going to open, we need to put our emotions to one side. When it's a more reasonable hour, I'll call the hospital and see how he's doing. Okay?"

Poppy nodded. "I'll do my best."

"You always do, and I'm sure he's going to be fine."

That seemed to make her feel better, and soon they were in the swing of things. Which was just as well, since the prediction that the diner would be busy was spot-on. All of them were rushed off their feet, but Lyra was the chief cook today, so she had a good reason for not venturing out into the crowd of people wanting any morsel of juicy gossip.

Lyra kept a plastic container by the grill to drop in food scraps, and it was already full, so she carried it to the larger trash bin. It wasn't where it usually sat, and there was one of the tablecloths they used at the wake draped over it. Flicking the material off and stomping on the lever to open it, she sighed heavily. Overflowing, there was no way it could take any more. Placing the container to one side, she pulled the liner up with a grunt. It was much heavier than usual. As she forced it over the rim, the recyclable material gave way. Food scraps dropped onto the floor, and something clanged against the tiles.

Mom tutted. "I hate that. People shouldn't fill them up so much."

"Even so, it shouldn't be that heavy," Lyra groaned at the mess. "I guess Leroy hadn't gotten around to emptying it before—"

Poppy hurried across the room. "What a disgusting mess. You're so busy, let me handle this."

Lyra waved her away. "No. I did this, so I'll clean it up. Could you get me the pan and brush though?"

The girl hesitated, clearly expecting that Lyra wouldn't dirty her hands this way, which made her wonder if she'd given the wrong impression. She was their boss, but she was hands-on in every aspect and would never expect her employees do something she wasn't prepared to do.

"It's fine, Poppy," Lyra told her, "You carry on serving. This won't take a minute." She pulled another bag from the roll and crouched to begin the unpleasant task.

Her fingers immediately touched something. Something very hard.

16

"What on earth is in here?" Removing wrinkled lettuce leaves and other scraps that would make it into the compost pile at the end of her garden, Lyra found a small cast-iron skillet. It didn't appear burnt. In fact, apart from having gross vegetables stuck to it, the thing looked in perfect condition. "I don't understand, this seems fine to me." She held it up. "I wonder who threw this out?"

Patricia leaned over Lyra's shoulder. "Why would a skillet be in with the food scraps anyway? Maybe Earl made a mistake when he was washing up."

Unloading the dishwasher, Earl's head jerked up, making his blonde ponytail bounce. "What did I do?"

"Did you throw out this skillet?"

Drying his hands on his apron, Earl came to look at the offending item. "No, ma'am." He shook his head emphatically. "I wouldn't throw out something like that unless I asked you or Leroy first."

Even after a few months working here, his nervousness hadn't left, and since he pretty much still asked permission for everything, Lyra believed him. His eyes pleaded with her, and he was definitely distressed about being asked such a thing. Despite having no other explanation, Lyra smiled.

"It's okay, Earl. Maybe it has a fault I can't see, and Leroy didn't want it anymore. All I ask is that we remember in the future that food scraps are kept separate to any other kind."

A look of relief swept across his face. "I'll remember. Shall I get the mop?"

"Yes, please." Lyra placed the skillet to one side while she finished picking up the rest of the trash. Tying up the bag, she handed it to Earl to take to the bigger trash bin outside, which Dan would wheel down to the garden at the end of the day.

"What are you going to do with the skillet? Shall I wash it up?" Poppy offered.

"Not just yet. I want to check it out first. They're expensive, so if I can salvage it, I will. If not, I'll put it in the other trash myself."

While Poppy went to serve the customers, Lyra took the pan to the sink. Mom followed and Lyra held it up so they could both look it over. "There's nothing wrong with it, is there?"

"Looks good to me too."

A thin reddish-brown sauce had stuck to the front edge, along with a bit of purple plastic and other unidentifiable bits. Lyra gulped. "Mom, what if it that isn't sauce?" she asked in a hushed voice.

"You can't think… Oh, my. Is it blood?" Mom whispered.

Carefully, Lyra placed it on a clean towel and washed her hands. Taking her phone out to the veranda, she dialed the police station. "I need to speak to the sheriff urgently. I think I found the weapon used to hit Leroy."

Officer Moore gasped. "He's out on a call, but I know he would want this information, so I'll contact him right away."

Lyra went back inside and moved the towel-wrapped

skillet to the table. Earl did dishes. Poppy collected orders from Mom as if everything was normal. Except it wasn't normal, and Mom looked as shook-up as she was.

It was maybe five minutes before the sheriff arrived—although it seemed longer. Lyra nodded to the towel. "I found this in the trash, and I don't think that's jam on the edge of it."

Walker slipped on gloves pulled from his pants pocket and gingerly unwrapped the offending pan. "It certainly looks like blood. I'll get a sample and see if matches Leroy's. Did you touch it?"

She grimaced. "Since I had no idea what it was, yes, I did pick it up. It was in the trash, and I only found out because the bag ripped when I pulled it out and everything spilled all over the floor."

He scratched his head. "I'll still get it dusted, but I don't know how we missed the trash."

"There were tablecloths on top of the bin," she offered lamely.

"It's not a good enough excuse, but that's not your problem. I would like to take a look at the rest of the contents the skillet was in with."

"Come outside. It's in the trash already because I hadn't considered that it was blood on the skillet when I cleaned the mess up."

He nodded and followed her. Cinnamon danced at his feet, but he ignored her, totally focused on the trash. Unceremoniously, he pulled out the offending bag, untied it, and in one movement dumped the contents on a patch of grass. On his haunches, he sifted through everything, a little at a time.

"What are you looking for exactly?"

"Nothing in particular, but if a person needs to get rid of evidence in a hurry, they might have mistakenly left something behind, or there may be more than one piece of evidence."

"I never thought of that."

"Since you aren't a member of the department, I don't know why you would." He sighed. "There's nothing here." Scooping it all back into the bag, he dropped it in the bin again. "I'll get that skillet checked out. Good work finding it and contacting me right away."

His praise was unexpected, and Lyra was suddenly tongue-tied. She followed him back into the diner where Poppy and Earl stood over the skillet, both pale.

"Was this really what kn-kn-knocked out Leroy?" Earl stuttered.

"We can't know for sure yet, but I think so." Walker replaced his filthy gloves with new ones.

"Lucky Lyra found it," Earl gave Lyra his awestruck look.

Mom nodded. "It was good luck, and bad luck for the person who did it."

Earl nodded enthusiastically. "I hope you get them, Sheriff, and lock them away forever."

"Thanks to Lyra, that just might happen." Walker patted him on the shoulder and left, taking the skillet, which was wrapped back up in the towel.

Still reeling from the sheriff talking her up, Lyra was lost in thought for a few moments and, when she snapped out of it, found Poppy and Earl watching her. "Right, let's get back to work. There are bound to be people waiting out front, and we don't need to mention this development," she told them firmly.

The younger members of her team hurried to comply.

"That was a little harsh," Mom said as she flipped pancakes.

"This whole business has me wound up tighter than a screw, but I shouldn't take it out on them," she acknowledged. "I guess it's knowing that someone came in here and hurt Leroy and they're out there somewhere. I don't want them to be alerted that we might have an important lead."

Mom smiled gently. "That's a good point, and I daresay you have a lot going on in that clever head of yours. Hopefully this will get sorted soon, then things might return to some form of normalcy."

Her words didn't fool Lyra. Mom could see how Walker affected her. The problem was she didn't know why. Another mystery that wouldn't get solved by her standing around.

Taking the stacked plates of pancakes, Lyra made her way to the table where Poppy was taking orders from the knitting club. Vanessa smiled at her daughter. "I see the sheriff's been in again. Was he here for work or pleasure?"

"Mom!" Poppy sent Lyra a pained glance.

Vanessa raised an eyebrow. "Can't I ask a simple question? You've been awfully snippy lately."

"When I'm at work you have to treat me differently," Poppy pleaded. "I can't join in the gossip."

"We do not gossip. Stop embarrassing me in front of my friends," Vanessa hissed.

Lyra stepped between them. "Poppy, could you get the next orders out? I'll take over here."

Red-faced, the young woman all but ran to the kitchen.

"I don't know what's got into her," Vanessa said stiffly.

"She's still very upset about what happened to Leroy," Lyra pointed out.

"We're all upset about that."

Vanessa didn't appear to have much empathy for her daughter which bothered Lyra. "They do work together and have become good friends."

"Any idea when he'll be back at work?" Carrie-Ann asked.

"Maybe in a week or so, if he's up to it. What can I get you, ladies?"

Lyra made sure that she was the one to deliver their coffees and pie and took the opportunity to ask after Arabelle.

"She's hardly out and about these days." Carrie-Ann tutted. "Naturally we've all been to check on her, but she won't have anyone inside the house."

"Why is that?"

"She's always been standoffish, and I think she's become a hermit because everyone got sick of her being so rude and obnoxious." Vanessa sniffed. "Still, we did our Christian duty and can report she is well."

"I got the impression that she'd been crying when I visited," Carrie-Ann added.

Vanessa rounded on her. "You never said anything about that."

"I didn't want to embarrass her."

"Then why say it now?"

"Because Lyra's good with people. Maybe she can find out what's wrong with her."

"Don't be foolish. Arabelle feeling sorry for herself is just a way to get attention."

"She doesn't like attention."

"Then why does she swan around making sure we all know where she is?"

"That was before, and it was only when she was near Rob."

The other ladies snickered.

Lyra tapped her order tablet to get their attention. "Are you saying that Arabelle and Rob were actually friends?"

"Oh, they were more than that."

"It was a long time ago," Carrie-Ann interrupted again. "And then there was Vanessa's little thing with Rob. That's another reason for Poppy to be so upset."

Vanessa glared. "That was years ago, and it meant nothing other than a few meals together."

Lyra was dumbfounded for the second time this morning, and Carrie-Ann smiled knowingly.

"What you must understand, dear, is that there aren't too many eligible men in Fairview. Rob stood head and shoulders over any of the ones we do have, so it's only natural that a few would be interested in him."

"He had his house and a business and always kept himself clean." Martha winked. "Hardly any grease under his nails at all."

The ding of the kitchen bell told Lyra that food was waiting to be delivered. "Excuse me," she told the group and hurried to collect the meals.

"I'm so sorry about Mom," Poppy said. "She has to discuss everything, even when it's personal. Unless it's about her."

"Don't worry about it. Moms are like that."

"Hey, I resent that." Mom grinned from the grill.

"It's just so embarrassing," Poppy added.

"Do you mean about her relationship with Mr. McKenna?"

Her chin wobbled. "That was actually a really good time in my life. He was so kind to me. A bit like the way Leroy is with me."

Lyra smiled. "A father figure like either of them would be a blessing."

"I knew you'd understand. We had so much fun together, but Mom spoiled it as she always does." Poppy gasped. "Not that Mom has a lot of male friends. As far as I know there was only Rob after my dad."

"I never thought otherwise," Lyra assured her. Vanessa's love life wasn't something she chose to contemplate. "Anyway, you have no need to be embarrassed about what your mom says. If you help my mom, I'll take their food out."

The young woman smiled gratefully, and since Vanessa was still being surly, it seemed it was the best call. Carrie-Ann paid her friend no mind at all, which was kind of funny. It must be nice to live in a world where what people said rolled off you like water, even those who were arguably hard to get on with.

That reminded her of Arabelle. It intrigued Lyra that maybe Arabelle also cared more for Rob than she would ever admit. Far pricklier than Vanessa, how could she possibly bring up the topic with Arabelle without causing offense? But if she didn't at least try, how else could she possibly get more information about Rob and what could have happened to him?

17

Things usually slowed down once breakfast was done, and thankfully, today was no exception. Lyra took the opportunity to contact the hospital and was told that Leroy was in a stable condition.

Next, she called Sheriff Walker. While she wanted to share the news about Leroy so he could convey the message when interviewing people, there was also the need to know if he had any more news on Leroy's attacker.

Disappointingly, the friendly voice of earlier this morning changed as soon as she asked. Surely it was a fair question, but he had nothing he could or would say about the matter other than no one had been caught yet and they were working hard to change that.

It sounded like something he read off a card, and though she was sure Walker was doing his best, this was personal. After Rob's death and Leroy's injury, she was frustrated and worried that there was no one in custody. After spending so much time with the two of them, she cared a great deal about seeing this through. And while she could do nothing more for Rob, she desperately needed to know, was she somehow the motive for hurting both men?

A physical pain clutched at her stomach. It wasn't too many months ago that she'd been through similar troubles and people had been hurt because of her. She couldn't bear it if something happened to anyone else. Had she made a mistake bringing Mom here?

"I'm going to see Leroy." The words were out before they were more than a conscious thought.

"Good idea. Then you can see for yourself how he's really doing," Patricia said.

"I hate to leave you to cope with lunch, but I think we'd all like a firsthand account, right?"

Poppy nodded enthusiastically, as did the others.

"Do you mind if I come?" Maggie asked. "It's not as though I can cook."

Lyra took off her apron and smiled. Maggie watched her the same way her mom did, and knew she was struggling. Quite frankly the company would be nice. "You're welcome to come. There are no orders waiting, so now is the best time. Are you sure you don't mind, Mom?"

"Not at all. With Poppy, Earl, and me, we have a great team. The customers will understand why there's nothing fancy when they know where you've gone."

As she was leaving, Poppy handed her a small posy of flowers.

"They're from Mom's garden." She spoke through quivering lips. "I asked her to bring them for the diner, but could you take them to Leroy and please give him our love?"

Lyra took the flowers and gave her a hug. "They're lovely, and don't worry, I'm sure he's going to be as good as new very soon."

"I hope so." Her big eyes shone with tears.

It was all Lyra could do not to shed a few herself. Relieved that Mom and the other two were holding down the fort, Lyra made up a box of cookies, and then she and Maggie set off for the hospital. Glad of each other's company, they drove the country lanes in peace until they got closer to Destiny.

"What will you tell him about last night?" Maggie asked.

"There's nothing to tell, except that the sheriff is working hard to find his attacker. What I find odd about this whole business is that both Rob and Leroy are nice men who don't appear to have any enemies. They both live, or lived, quiet lives, and while they're friendly enough, as far as I know they keep to themselves most of the time when they aren't working."

"I was thinking the same thing. Leroy works long hours, and Rob did too. If he wasn't working at the garage, he was pottering around at his home."

Lyra nodded. "Then there's the fact that whoever hurt Leroy clearly wasn't aiming to kill him. Which means it had to be a warning. If that's so, what did he see or know that would warrant it?"

"Surely he would have said something if he knew who'd killed Rob?"

"Exactly. Which makes me think it wasn't about that."

Maggie sighed. "Hopefully Leroy has some answers."

Lyra pulled into the car park, and once inside, they were directed to Leroy's room. He was sitting up in bed reading the paper and grinned when he saw them.

"Now aren't you a wonderful sight to see this morning."

Lyra smiled, although she had a lump in her throat. Dark under the eyes, Leroy had a bandage covering most of his hair. "We feel the same about you. That was a horrible scare you gave us last night. How are you doing?"

"I won't lie." He touched the bandage. "My head aches a little."

Maggie snorted. "No surprises there, my friend."

"These are from Poppy and her mom." Lyra handed him the posy.

He grinned again. "She's a sweet girl. Always worrying about me. Why don't you take a seat?"

They sat one on either side of his bed. Lyra placed the box of cookies on the small cubby where a water jug and cup sat.

Leroy raised an eyebrow. "Please tell me that's what I think it is."

"Well now that depends on what you were hoping for, but it is a little treat if you're allowed. When will you be able to go home?"

He licked his lips. "According to the nurse, the doctor should be by soon. Everyone's been very nice, and I had a visit from the sheriff already this morning."

"Really? He was in the diner first thing doing a check before he'd let me open. He must have come straight after."

"He told me you were all working hard to get the diner up and running again. There must have been one heck of a mess after last night. Sorry to leave you in the lurch, but I'll be back as soon as I can."

Lyra snorted. "It's not like you're intentionally unable to work, and you're not to give it another thought until you're feeling right and cleared by the doctor."

"Yes, ma'am."

Maggie put a hand on his arm. "Won't you be scared to come back to the diner?"

Leroy's' mouth pursed for a second. "Until they find out who put me in here, I'll be wary, but not scared."

"Because they didn't want to kill you?"

"Doesn't seem as if that was the point of the exercise. Either that or they couldn't follow through."

Lyra grimaced. "Do you actually have any enemies?"

He shrugged. "I came to Fairview to start a new life, and I

can't think of anyone in town that I've rubbed the wrong way."

That was an interesting answer. Could Leroy have annoyed someone enough to follow him here? It seemed a bit far-fetched. "Maybe you saw something you shouldn't have."

"It's a small town. There aren't too many secrets."

"I wouldn't be so sure about that," Maggie muttered.

"What do you mean?"

Lyra caught Maggie's eyes and shook her head. There would be time to discuss all that when Leroy was feeling better. Before Maggie could come up an answer, the doctor arrived.

"Good morning, Mr. Burns, and family?"

"We're friends and co-workers," Lyra explained.

The doctor ran a finger along the notes on a file he carried, then he shone a penlight in Leroy's eyes and made him follow the light back and forth as well as conducting a couple more tests. "You're doing extremely well, and while we don't take these things lightly, I see no point in keeping you here. You can go home, as long as you take things easy for a few days and get in touch with the hospital if your symptoms worsen. The nurse will provide instructions for changing the dressings and getting the stitches removed."

"Thank you, Doctor. I'll be certain to follow your advice."

"We'll make sure of it," Lyra assured the doctor, not believing Leroy for one moment. "And we'll get him home safely."

The doctor nodded. "Good, and please note there's no driving for at least twenty-four hours, Mr. Burns. Any questions?"

Leroy frowned. "I'm sure I should ask something, but nothing springs to mind."

"That's quite usual in these circumstances. Please ring the hospital if you think of something later. You can get dressed while you wait for the nurse to bring the necessary paper-work and a prescription for pain meds, as well as a dose to see you through the next few hours. They're not particularly strong, but you should keep on top of them for the next day or so."

Leroy thanked him, and Lyra handed him a bag. "I don't have a key for your house, otherwise I would have brought you clean clothes, but I did borrow a shirt off Dan, as I remembered yours was covered in blood."

"Trust you to think of that little detail. I think my shirt is going straight in the trash." He took his clothes into the attached bathroom.

18

He wasn't gone long, and when the nurse was finished, they took the walk to the car park slowly, where Maggie insisted he take the passenger seat.

Leroy sat back with a sigh. "They were very good to me, but I'm so glad to be going home. I'm also very thankful you stopped by and don't mind giving me a ride. It sure beats taking a cab."

"Don't be silly." Lyra tutted. "It's a lovely day for a drive, and we wanted to make sure you were okay. Plus, I must admit it was good to hear what the doctor had to say, otherwise I would have been worried you were coming home too early."

He grinned. "It's been a long time since anyone cared that much about me. Like you heard, all I have is a mild concussion."

Lyra glanced at him. Clearly another reminder was necessary. "I also heard him say that you can't take these things lightly. Concussions can hang around for a while, and you are not to come back to work until you're 100 percent better. Are we clear, Leroy?"

He gave a wry grin. "I get the point. The pain isn't too bad, but I must confess that my head is still a little fuzzy, and I don't think I could stand for long anyway."

"Thank you for being honest, and it's good the pain is bearable."

White around his mouth, Lyra knew Leroy hurt more than he was likely to admit, but at least he recognized his limitations. Frustrated that the culprit hadn't being caught yet, she wouldn't upset Leroy by going on about it today. Instead, she wore her game face. The one generally employed when she was interviewing stars who had something that needed brushing under the carpet.

"It's only been a few hours since it happened, and your body's dealing with what it's been through. There is no hurry to come back to work, and rest assured that you will be paid for the whole time."

He squirmed in his seat. "I'm not so worried about the money. How will you manage with the diner?"

Lyra snorted. "Well, I can cook a little, and I have run a kitchen, so I think we'll be okay."

Leroy laughed, then groaned. "Sorry, I'm not thinking clear."

"I'm not surprised. You were out cold, and there was a lot of blood." She mentally kicked herself for mentioning it that way.

He turned a little to face her. "It's weird not knowing what actually happened to me or why. I was humming along to the music, loading the dishwasher, and the next minute there was a sharp pain on the back of my head, and my knees buckled. I saw the floor getting closer and nothing after that. What do you make of it?"

She shot him a glance, and he seemed intent on an answer. "I distinctly recall locking the front door before taking the last plate of food to the house. Whoever did this didn't come that way."

"I would have noticed anyone coming in the veranda door," Leroy pointed out.

She slapped the steering wheel. "Which means they were already inside and waited until you were alone."

"That's creepy," Maggie stated from the backseat. "Who have you annoyed, Leroy?"

"Me? Like I said earlier, I can't think of anyone who has enough beef with me to get physical over it."

"Hmmm. So, you do have some enemies then?" Lyra pressed.

He shrugged. "We all have people who don't see our way in things, but I think enemies is a little harsh."

Lyra nodded. "For me it still points to Phillip McKenna."

"You'll get no arguments here. It appears he hates the town because of his father and wants someone to pay for his misery. I guess I was the easy, or maybe the only, target he could reach."

"I agree. It's obvious that he wanted to hurt me, and perhaps he felt that by not having a chef, I'd have to shut the diner until you were well." Lyra bounced her ideas around, and Leroy ran with them.

"Unless he wanted me dead, so you'd have to close permanently."

"Then why didn't he make sure of it? Sorry, that was tactless. And the issue with that is he knows I can cook." Lyra frowned, not sure what Phillip did know about any of them. "At least, he knows I had a show."

"He might not appreciate how tenacious you are and thinks he could scare you out of town, and when that didn't work, he attacked Leroy," Maggie spoke passionately.

Lyra nodded at Maggie in the mirror. "The problem with

all this is that his real beef is with Dan. Hurting Leroy doesn't affect the bequeathing of the garage."

"Dan's a big guy." Leroy pointed out. "If McKenna is the coward who hit me, maybe he was too scared to tackle Dan."

"You might be right. Still, I can't see how he gets anything out of this except to pay me back for holding the after-function for Rob. You being injured won't get him the garage."

"That's true. He really didn't want the wake or to lose the garage." Leroy suddenly smirked. "Guess he not only lucked out on both accounts, but he hurt himself too."

"In what way?"

"He loves the way I cook his steak, but he's hardly going to come in and eat at the diner now if he knows we think he hit me." Leroy closed his eyes, the grin stuck in place.

Maggie snorted. "Good job. He can starve for all I care."

"I'm hoping that after the will reading on Monday, he'll leave town." Lyra sighed. "Only, he still has to organize selling or renting the house and sorting all Rob's effects. Unless he's been doing that as well as harassing us, he could be here for days if not weeks. I hate the idea of him living so close and not knowing what he's up to."

"I know what you mean. I could hardly sleep last night." Maggie grimaced. "I kept thinking he was outside somewhere looking at another way to get in."

Lyra shuddered, but a snore from beside her made her grin. "Clearly that's not a problem for some of us."

Maggie giggled. "I can help out in the diner until he's feeling well enough."

"Thanks, Mags. If Mom helps me in the kitchen, then you could help Poppy."

"You don't look as happy as I thought you would by my offer. Is it my cooking skills? Because I wouldn't force them on anybody."

Lyra laughed softly. "Sorry. I am grateful and pretty sure

Mom will step up. With your help, that's a huge worry off my shoulders."

"I sense a but coming."

Lyra lowered her voice further, and Maggie leaned forward to hear. "I keep thinking about Phillip McKenna and what he has on his agenda for the will reading. With no proof it was Phillip who attacked Leroy, the sheriff isn't about to arrest him."

"More's the pity."

Lyra nodded. "Which means the reading of the will is going to happen. If Dan wants the garage, I honestly think Phillip should let him have it. Only, I don't think he'll give in easily. Will Dan fight for it as he should, or would it be safer not to?"

"Hah! Dan can take care of himself. He's had army training, and besides, Leroy made sense that Phillip is too scared to try anything with him."

There was no point in going on about being worried for everyone's safety, and she didn't want Leroy to wake up and hear them talking about it. For now, all Lyra could do was keep the diner running and support Dan. But she would do all this with one eye on the man next door.

When they returned after dropping Leroy at his cottage, the kitchen was a shambles. Lyra was exhausted just looking at it for the second time in a day.

"We concentrated on feeding people and clearing tables," Patricia blurted as soon as they were in the door. "We'll have this under control in a jiffy, so don't stress about it. How is Leroy?"

Poppy and Earl stopped scraping dishes and loading the dishwasher to listen, and Dan came in from emptying the trash.

"He's doing so well that the doctor let us bring him home.

He'll be out of action for at least a few days, but he was so happy to be in familiar surroundings."

"That's wonderful news!" Patricia hugged her and Maggie.

"Thank goodness," said Poppy. "I'll be glad to do extra hours until he's back on his feet."

"Me too," Earl added.

"Thanks, guys. Maggie's also offered to lend a hand, so I think we'll be just fine. There is the matter of tomorrow. At mid-morning Dan and I have an appointment, so you'll be short-handed again because Maggie wants to come. If we have happy customers, then I don't care how it looks out here."

"Oh yes, I'd forgotten about that," Patricia admitted.

"I hadn't." Dan grimaced.

"With Lyra by your side, you're in good hands. And I'll be there too," Maggie assured him.

"I appreciate the moral support." His smile didn't reach his eyes.

19

Dan paced the kitchen, glancing at his watch every few seconds.

"Lucky there's no carpet," Lyra told him while putting the finishing touches to three plates of eggs Benedict.

"I can't sit down; my stomach's in a knot."

Maggie handed him a coffee. "Nothing bad is going to happen. Karl will simply tell you what's what."

"Except Rob's son will be there, and I feel guilty about taking his inheritance."

Patricia waved a finger at him. "You can stop that right now. This was Rob's wish. Isn't that more important to you than Phillip's meanness?"

He shrugged. "Putting the blame on him seems an easy way out."

"Out of what?" Maggie asked.

"The guilt."

"Fine." Maggie shook her head. "Go ahead and make yourself miserable. Better yet, why not say no to a once-in-a-lifetime opportunity? After all, no one's twisting your arm to take the garage."

Poppy gasped at Maggie, and hurriedly took the plates of food out to the diner.

Unable to bear what Dan's angst was doing to them, Lyra stepped in. "There's simply no point in stressing over this until all the cards are on the table. We're early, but why don't we take a slow walk to Karl's office now? The fresh air might help everyone's nerves."

"Yes, you go." Patricia waved them away. "Poppy and I have this under control."

Lyra hesitated at the door. "The breakfast rush is over, but are you sure you can handle things until I get back?"

"I've been practicing so I could help out if necessary, and after yesterday, I think Leroy would approve of me stepping in for an hour. In fact, I phoned him a little while ago. He said he's feeling much better and is sure I'm doing just fine. I didn't argue, because we all know I'm not a patch on him, but needs must, right?"

"There's only been praise coming from the customers, so don't sell yourself short, Mom." Lyra removed her apron and hung it on the peg. "Alright, I'll be back as soon as I can."

They went via the diner, forgetting that the knitting club were in.

"How's Leroy?"

"He's fine, Vanessa. We picked him up yesterday, and Mom phoned him earlier. He'll be resting this week instead of working and just needs some quiet to heal properly." Lyra hoped by saying it loud and firmly enough, the women would leave Leroy alone and not fuss over him unless he wanted them to.

Vanessa raised an eyebrow. "Poppy told me. Concussions can have complications. Why I heard of someone in Cozy Hollow who had that very thing and never went back to work, so don't you make him come back too early."

Lyra bit back a snappy remark that she had no intention

of making Leroy come back until he was healthy again, and forced a smile. "I wouldn't dream of it."

"There's something different with my eggs." Carrie-Ann poked her meal with a knife.

"You don't like them?"

"Actually, I prefer them this way. Did you make them?"

Lyra nodded.

"Then you better show Leroy how you do it when he returns, because I'm a convert."

With a genuine smile, Lyra hurried out the door. Leroy's eggs were just fine, but she could hardly be annoyed by such a compliment. Plus, the less she engaged with her customers, the less likely she'd let it slip where they were headed. As far as she knew, Vanessa and her fellow knitters were unaware of the will being read today, and she'd like to keep it that way for Dan's sake. They'd find out soon enough if he did get the garage, but that wasn't a given.

"It was all I could do not to tell her to mind her own business." Maggie snorted beside her. "Lucky they don't know what we're doing this morning."

"Shhh. I'm surprised they don't," Lyra whispered, but she grinned at their similar train of thought. "Not much gets past those four."

Dan met them at the corner, hands thrust into his pockets and a line etched into his forehead as deep as a chasm. As they got closer to the lawyers, his steps slowed and he lagged behind them. Maggie rolled her eyes, but Lyra gave her a warning glance.

"We have plenty of time," she muttered. Dan was only delaying the inevitable, and with the prospect of seeing Phillip again, she couldn't blame him.

The receptionist ushered them straight into Karl's office, and he jumped from his chair to shake their hands. Phillip McKenna was already there, sitting stiffly in front of the heavy wooden desk.

"What are you two doing here?" he protested, when he saw Lyra and Maggie. "This is a private meeting."

"They're here with me," Dan growled. "Is that a problem?"

Karl put up a hand. "Let's keep this civil, gentleman. Mr. McKenna, as I explained, both parties are allowed witnesses."

"Then they better keep quiet." He turned away and crossed his arms.

"Ladies, if you'd take a seat at the back, we can get started. Mr. Best, please sit here." Karl patted the back of a matching chair to Phillip's, which was a few feet away from him.

Lyra decided the space between them was a very good idea.

"Thank you for coming," Karl acknowledged both men. "Please bear with me while I read the legal part, then I'll answer any questions as soon as that's done."

He immediately launched into the will without getting confirmation, which was another wise move in Lyra's opinion. Dan listened intently, as did Lyra and Maggie, while Phillip studied his fingernails. Clearly nothing in the will surprised him, but it did tug at her heart strings.

"No matter what he may think of me, I love my son Phillip and wish him nothing but happiness. While he is entitled to everything his mom and I have, I lived frugally and believe there is plenty to share. Some time ago I decided that the garage needs to go to someone who has a love for cars as I do. Clearly once I'm gone, what happens to my possessions is of no consequence, yet it gives me great pleasure to hand over the thing that kept me going after losing my family to Daniel Best.

Our friendship is of months and not years but is no less mean-

ingful to me. I have no doubt this is a shock and I apologize to him for not discussing the matter.

Dan you know more about engines than you think. You have a gift and it shouldn't be wasted. While I can't deny that you are good with your hands, and could do most things, that is not the same as doing what you love. At least give it a try for a year or two. If you hate it, then sell the garage and buy something that suits you better.

I do not want there to be any animosity over my decision and that is why there is a stipulation about not contesting the will. If Phillip contests the will and loses everything I own will be given away except the garage which will still go to Daniel Best.

I'm sorry if this upsets you, Phillip, but this is what I want. My only regret is not seeing you and telling you that I love you."

When Karl turned the last page over and sat back, Maggie, Lyra, and Dan wiped hastily at their eyes.

He gave them a moment before continuing. "Thank you for your patience. Mr. McKenna had a copy of the will sent to him by his father a month ago and has already raised a few questions which I have addressed and need not concern you, Mr. Best. For my part, I can assure all parties that the will is legal, and unless contested, it will be put into place as soon as practical. These things can take months, but I have the documents ready to sign if you are both in agreement."

"You know how I feel," Phillip stated harshly.

"Yes, Mr. McKenna. While I appreciate you think your father was misguided, you also know the consequences of contesting his wishes."

Phillip snatched the paper from the desk and, using his own pen, signed with a flourish. He thrust the pen into his top pocket, glared at Dan, then marched out of the room, banging the door shut behind him.

For a moment everyone but the lawyer sat in stunned silence. Karl waited patiently for the outcome to sink in. The fact that Phillip didn't want Dan to have the garage was nullified by Rob's condition that he not contest it.

Lyra moved to Dan's side and squeezed his shoulder. "This is what Rob wanted. Go ahead and sign the paper."

After a brief hesitation and with a shaking hand, Dan took the pen Karl offered and signed his name. A little pale, he sat back and released a long breath. "This is surreal."

Karl reached across and shook his hand. "Congratulations, Dan. I'd like to alleviate your worries if I can. When Rob asked me to change his will, he was sound of mind and, as Lyra said, he truly wanted you to take over the garage. I appreciated that you hadn't known each other for very long, so I talked to him at some length to make sure it wasn't something he might regret. Not once did he waver in his decision. In fact, he was very emphatic."

"But why me?"

"Because he knew you would appreciate it and that you also had a love for machinery and—as he called it— tinkering."

Dan managed a crooked smile. "Thanks, Karl. It does help, but I still feel odd about how this came to be."

"That's natural. Give it some time to sink in and then try to enjoy the challenges of owning a business in a small town." He gave a wry grin. "I have a feeling you'll be very popular. Here are the keys. It's a little early hand them over, but I always advise people who receive property to change all the locks. It's a standard procedure, but also necessary."

He didn't say so, but Lyra could hear in his voice that, with the bad blood over this, changing locks was a priority. Considering everything that had happened, she agreed wholeheartedly.

"Oh. Sure. I can do that myself." Dan finally stood, still looking a little blank.

"Rob did say that you were a great handyman. I hope that translates into fixing vehicles."

"I learned a lot in the army, but thanks to him, I have a far better knowledge of engines than when I arrived in town," Dan admitted. "Although, he probably forgot more than I know."

The attempt at humor was a good sign, which Karl seemed to pick up on.

"If it makes a difference, Rob was no fool and must have trusted you were good enough to run the garage as he did."

"Thanks, Karl. You can be sure I'll give it my best shot."

They shook hands again, and when they got outside, Dan breathed a large sigh. "I didn't imagine for one minute that it would go off without a hitch."

"Me either," Maggie admitted. "Phillip looked like he wanted to smash something."

Dan gave a lop-sided grin. "At a guess, I'd say that something was me."

"I wonder what would have happened if he had contested it," Maggie pondered. "Karl obviously didn't want to share what those conditions were."

"Yeah, it must be something Phillip wasn't willing to put into play," Dan agreed.

"Let's not worry about that. He didn't, so you can move on." Lyra nudged him, just as curious but wanting Dan to appreciate the moment. "You have a garage!"

"It's unbelievable." The bright grin gave way to another frown. "I've never owned a business, and I've got no idea how to run one. Rob never touched on bookwork, and why would I think to ask when there was no clue that this was on the horizon?"

"Don't stress about bookwork. I can help with that," Maggie offered. "I can organize your accounts and make phone calls—when I'm not working for Lyra."

"That's a fantastic idea." Lyra may as well have kept silent for all the notice Dan paid her.

His features softened as he gazed at Maggie. "I'd be very grateful."

"Sure, you will," she teased. "You can put me on your payroll once you satisfy your first customer."

The two of them burst into laughter, and Lyra wondered if they knew what a cute couple they made. And, if they didn't right now, how long would it take until they did realize. Most likely Vanessa and her group would point it out—if Mom didn't.

20

To Lyra's relief, the knitting club ladies were gone when they got back, and the place was relatively quiet. And messy, yet again. It must have gotten busy once they left, and Lyra grabbed a few plates on the way to the kitchen.

"Dan and I will clean up out here," Maggie offered.

"Thanks, it looks like Mom and Poppy are taking a break." She nodded gratefully to Earl, who was pouring coffee for the only two customers, and sure enough found Mom and Poppy drinking coffee at the kitchen table.

"Thank goodness you're back, and none too soon," Patricia groaned. "Goodness, I don't know what got into the town today, considering we had that big rush this morning, but they were here one after the other asking all kinds of questions along with every order. Honestly, poor Poppy was like a broken record."

"I guess once the word spread that Leroy was home, they were curious all over again. Thanks for holding down the fort. Why don't you head back to the house and have a proper rest before the lunch crowd fronts up?"

Patricia stood with a wince. "No need to tell me twice.

My feet are killing me. Poppy and Earl were awesome by the way. They kept the cups filled and sold just about everything in the cabinet. Although, that could be because I'm a lot slower at cooking than you or Leroy."

"It would have been worth the wait," Lyra assured her.

Mom kissed her cheek. "That's very sweet to say, and I didn't hear anything bad. How did you get on, Dan?"

He stacked more plates beside the ones Maggie brought in, and shrugged. "Fine, I guess. The garage is mine, and Phillip McKenna isn't disputing it."

"Really?" Patricia chuckled. "Well, there you go. The man must have found some sense, and isn't it wonderful to have things sorted this quickly? Now you can move on and create your new business persona."

Lyra flinched at the idea. She didn't want Dan to move on at all, but she kept this to herself. He deserved his chance, and she wouldn't hold him back. "It will be exciting to view the place for the first time as yours."

"The paperwork has to be filed, but would you mind if I went to the garage today?" he asked. "I haven't really had a good look around on my own, and I'd like to get the locks changed as Karl suggested."

Dan's eyes shone brightly, showing how much this meant to him. Finally accepting that he was a business owner, he could allow himself to be excited by the challenge.

"Go right ahead, and while you're there, it might pay to take an inventory and check on any clients who may be booked in."

His eyes widened. "Shoot! I never gave anything like that a second thought."

Lyra laughed. "I didn't say it to make you panic. Everyone knows that Rob passed away, so they'll understand it will take some time to sort things out.

Maggie wiped her hair back from her face as she emptied

the dishwasher. "If there's any bookwork pending, put it to one side and I'll come down tomorrow to see if I can sort you out in the short term."

"Thanks, Mags. I'd appreciate that. Hopefully once I understand how things work, I can handle it on my own. After all, Rob did, so I should be able to."

He did his best to sound positive, and the women shared a smile behind his back as he left like a man on a mission.

"I'd say he won't be doing a lot of work around here from today," Maggie said sadly.

"That's true, but I don't want to think about how much I'll miss him around the place. Having him on hand to remodel the house and diner as well as fix almost anything, all the while with a smile, has been a blessing. It's beyond hard to imagine being without him."

"He'll miss being here too."

"I know, Mags, but we'd have to be blind not to see that he wants this, and we can't stand in his way. This is a huge gift, and while he's not convinced that he should have this opportunity, I believe he's more than capable of making the garage work."

"He is determined when he sets his mind on something." Maggie tilted her head. "Sometimes you have no idea what you really want until it's in your face."

Lyra raised an eyebrow. Was Maggie speaking from experience? And did she mean jobwise or in regard to Dan? Both reasons intrigued her. It would be hard to do without Dan, but Maggie moving on was untenable. It was best to get into some work and not dwell on where all this might lead.

Maggie finished cleaning up the diner while Lyra quickly made blueberry muffins and cooked a hearty chicken soup before the lunch crowd arrived. After her break, Patricia diced the vegetables and Poppy served at the counter. Instantly, Lyra was calmer.

This kind of cooking took little thought, and her mind wandered. Her friends from her old restaurant had phoned a couple of days ago to see how everything was going. Along with Kaden, they all kept in touch every week in the form of a quick text or a video chat. Naturally, talking to any of them made her think of the differences in running an upmarket place compared to the diner.

The best thing to come out of her lifestyle change was realizing that she didn't need all the glitz and glamor of a life she had never really been comfortable with. She was truly happy here. Of course, with Rob dying, Phillip being so horrible, and Leroy's attack, the shine on Fairview was somewhat diminished. Thank goodness Dan was having a little good luck.

Just then, Poppy came racing into the kitchen, pale as flour. "Rob's son is here, and he wants steak again."

"Is he just." Lyra stirred the soup and lowered the temperature. Wiping her hands on a towel, she took the muffins out of the oven and set them to cool. Patricia and Maggie stared as she walked casually into the diner. Little did they know how much effort it took to do so.

Phillip McKenna sat at the corner table with a book.

"Mr. McKenna, I believe you would like a rare steak the way Leroy makes them."

He took his time, carefully placing a piece of paper into the book before closing it and looking up at her. "That's right. Is there a problem?"

"You clearly don't see anything wrong with your request."

His eyes narrowed. "The only thing odd here it that an order doesn't usually require the cook to come check on it unless it's something out of the ordinary."

Lyra made an impatient sound. "While there's nothing unusual about rare steak, I do find it strange that you would choose to come back here when you are aware of the circumstance behind Leroy not being able to work."

He frowned. "The police did fill me in on the details, but you're still open, so I'm not sure why there's any issue."

She crossed her arms. "Since you're here after causing a ruckus over holding your father's wake, I guess you had an alibi for when Leroy was hit on the back of his head?"

"Are you suggesting I'm the one who hit Leroy?" he scoffed.

"I'm asking if you did."

He raised an eyebrow. "Listen, while I appreciate the candor behind your accusation, I assure you that I did not touch Leroy. During the celebration, I was at my father's place going through his things as I have done since I arrived —which is why I eat here. If I trusted that the ridiculously large amount of food in the fridge was recent, I can assure you I'd eat at my father's house. The fact that Leroy cooks my steak to perfection is also a drawcard."

Although there was initially a heavy dose of sarcasm lacing his reply, he did sound sincere. Only Lyra couldn't picture Rob stocking his freezer, because he ate most of his main meals at the diner. "I suppose while you were going over things at the house, you were seething at our gathering next door."

He shrugged. "You got me there. Yes, I was annoyed, but there was never anything I could do about it, right? Not when you have most of the town wrapped around your little finger, including the law."

"Except to ruin the evening," she reminded him, choosing to ignore the dig about the sheriff.

Phillip shrugged. "Again, not guilty. Now, am I going to get my steak today, or do I have to eat elsewhere?"

A silence loaded with dislike filled the space between them.

"Do you want fries with that?"

He nodded. "And two eggs, over easy."

Two tables of other customers muttered amongst themselves, and Lyra resolved to stifle any more drama in her diner.

"Coming right up." She marched back to the kitchen and held her hand up as soon as she saw the others' horrified glances. "Don't say a word."

Poppy, completely ignoring her, blurted, "After everything he's done, we can't feed him."

"Like he said, we can't prove it." Lyra slapped a steak onto the grill and threw a scoop of fries into the deep fryer. This would be the first meal in her life that she didn't make with love.

And that's when Mom stepped up. "Everybody calm down. We're all angry about the situation, but let's get through it as best we can. I'll take out the food when it's ready. Poppy, you carry on serving everyone else and leave Mr. McKenna to me. Maggie, it would be best if you help Lyra in here."

No one argued because it made perfect sense to keep the angriest of them away from a man whose very presence made the air hum with disapproval.

Lyra's heart didn't return to normal until Mom informed her that Phillip had gone. Just his being here had affected them all, but she was more worried about one of them in particular.

"That's a relief. Is Poppy okay?"

"She will be now. I guess he wasn't as hungry as he thought or the looks from other customers finally got to him, because he asked for a container for half of his steak. He also left behind his book. I found it on the chair beside him."

"Put it behind the counter, he's bound to call back for it." The thought wasn't appealing, but Lyra had no intention of chasing after him or forcing one of her staff to take it to Rob's house.

"I think you're right." Patricia rubbed the worn leather cover. "It looks very old, doesn't it? Maybe it was one of Rob's. I remember he used to have an amazing collection."

"He sure did and was happy to show them to me. They weren't my cup of tea, but I bet some of them are worth a great deal," Maggie added.

Lyra was walking past her mom when something caught her eye. "Wait a minute. That piece of paper sticking out the top like a bookmark—it's got the garage logo on it."

Patricia handed her the book, and Lyra slipped the paper from the pages. Carefully, she unfolded it and saw that it was an old-school handwritten receipt for repairs to a car. The registration was one she recognized, since it was parked in the drive next door. "This is for Phillip's car. Rob must have worked on it before he died."

Maggie peered over her shoulder. "That means Phillip could have been in Fairview the day of his father's death."

Lyra nodded. "We need to find out exactly the cause of death."

"Didn't the police already tell you that he had a heart attack?"

"That's right, but the sheriff also said that something was ingested which triggered it."

Poppy grew paler. "What does that mean?"

"Rob ate or drank something which affected his blood pressure. It must be written down somewhere what that was. Other than the sheriff, and the doctor, Phillip must know because of the autopsy. Herbs were mentioned, and I want to know what they were."

"Don't get in trouble by upsetting the sheriff," Poppy pleaded.

"I'll do my best not to, but I can't let it go. Not when any of us could be at risk because we still don't know what the murderer's motive is."

"But aren't you scared that the murderer could be close by?" Poppy's voice was almost a whisper.

Patricia hugged the girl and gave Lyra a meaningful glance. "It's all right, dear. You're safe with us."

Lyra hoped she was right. For all their sakes.

21

The more she thought about it, the less Lyra wanted to ask Phillip about the autopsy report. It wasn't likely that he'd willingly discuss anything with her. But there was another way.

The kitchen was closed, so Lyra was waiting for the last few customers to leave and took the time to research herbs that could affect blood pressure. While it wouldn't be a good look on her browser history, she forgot any worries about that when she found exactly what she was looking for. St Johns Wort and Ginseng worked against Beta Blockers. Now all she had to do was find out who grew them.

A knock at the back door startled her. It was only Dan and Maggie. Relieved, she let them in and explained about the herbs and finding the receipt left behind by Phillip McKenna.

"That's ironic, we were looking over things in the office and thought you might be interested in this." He placed a couple of books on the table and tapped the top one. "I found this tucked at the back of the register, which I might add was empty."

It was the same size as the receipt, and when she opened to the first page, she found carbon copies of the same type of receipts. Quickly, Lyra flipped to the back of the book. "The last receipt copy matches this one! "We need to call the sheriff."

While Lyra made the call, Cinnamon nosed her food near the door. With a heavy sigh, the beagle turned and went to curl up in her bed on a corner of the verandah. It was unusual for the beagle to be so lazy at this time of day, and she resolved to get her to the vet as soon as she could.

Leaving a message with the officer on duty, Lyra was drawn back to the book. She studied several pages, then returned to the page which was similar to the receipt. Thank goodness she'd decided to look at this before Walker confiscated it, and that Dan had found the book, because there was something so glaringly obvious her heart skipped a beat. "Look at this, guys. The writing is different in the book to the receipt we found!"

Maggie peered over her shoulder. "It looks okay to me. Mr. B Brown paid cash."

"Exactly, so no one can trace them and it's a good forgery, but look at the way g curls on the word sluggish – the reason for it needing to be fixed."

"Oh, yes. Though forgery sounds a little dramatic. Other customers paid cash and perhaps Rob had someone helping him that day," Maggie suggested.

"While that's true about the cash, it is unlikely that anyone else worked for Rob because Dan spent a lot of time with him and the subject surely would have come up." Lyra raised an eyebrow for confirmation.

Dan nodded. "He never mentioned it and I certainly never saw anyone working at the garage except Rob."

Satisfied she was on the right track, Lyra worked backward through the book again, only slower. "I don't see any others in that handwriting. Wait!"

"What did you find?" Dan leaned in eagerly.

Lyra's heartbeat quickened. "Another receipt this time to clean the carburetor. The name is P. Smith, and it was paid by cash, but that's Phillip's car registration. "

Dan leaned even closer, his head almost touching Maggie's. "They both have Phillip's car registration details, and this date means Phillip McKenna had his car fixed two days before Rob died."

"Exactly. Rob couldn't have recognized him, otherwise he would have mentioned it."

"I'm sure he would have told me." Dan put a finger to his temple. "My head's about to explode. When you add on a fake receipt the day he died, which was for something that would have been fixed by a new carburetor a few days earlier, what does this really mean?"

Lyra added that to her mental list of Philipp's innocence and waved the loose receipt. "Whoever wrote this up, and it clearly wasn't Rob, didn't know that Phillip had already been in to the garage. The forger wanted Phillip to look guilty if Rob's death was deemed suspicious. Meanwhile, Phillip didn't want anyone to know he was here."

"Which means he could have done it after all," Maggie said in an *I told you so* voice. "And how could he not recognize his own son?"

Lyra's cheeks burned. "I don't think he's guilty—of murder, but I am an idiot. Rob mentioned something about a stranger coming by and asking a lot of questions, which I told the sheriff and he dismissed. Rob hadn't seen his son for years and didn't even have a recent photo of him. According to Rob the stranger had a beard and Phillip is clean shaven, which is probably why no one else commented on him being here before. I should have remembered something so important. And it proves my point because there would be no point in going to the trouble to disguise himself and then leave a bogus receipt lying around."

"It does seem odd," Maggie mused. "A guilty person would be more inclined to get rid of the evidence than carry it around with them."

Dan shook his head several times. "But who could have staged it to look like this?"

"And more importantly, why?" Maggie added.

"It's bugging me because there are so many clues, but I still can't see the complete connection between them."

"You will," Dan assured her.

Lyra felt the pressure to solve this and soon. There was no way they could move on from Rob's death until they figured this out. Someone wanted Phillip to take the fall, and as much as she didn't like the man, that wasn't right.

Not long after this epiphany, Sheriff Walker arrived on his own, at the veranda door, still in uniform. Once Lyra let him in, he studied the group for a moment.

"You left a message that you had some important evidence."

Lyra poured him fresh coffee while she outlined the events and handed over the plastic bag she'd placed the book in. "Here's the book, and this is the receipt we found inside it. I'm sorry, but when Mom gave it to me, I didn't think to worry about fingerprints, and I've gone over it a couple of times. I don't believe Phillip left the receipt. I think it was planted in the book by someone who felt sure we would find it and put two and two together. If you check the car registration numbers on both receipts you'll notice they are identical. That's Phillip's car, but the names are different. Then we have the dates. The first is two days before Rob died, while the second is the day of his death."

Walker didn't answer but took a gulp of the hot liquid

before pulling on gloves and taking the items out of the bag.

Dan watched over his shoulder. "Regardless of Phillip leaving the receipt or not, it took a lot of nerve for him to stay in town, but a darn sight more to come by the diner for the same meal that Leroy fixed."

Walker sighed. "Despite what we all know you expect to be the outcome of this, Dan, I can only talk to him about being in town when he said he wasn't. There's no way we can say that he murdered Rob because of timing. Even with this evidence."

Lyra's frustration boiled over. "You're missing the point. Rob ate at home or here, and sometimes the women in the knitting club took him meals. Those are the perfect opportunities for someone to slip him something, right?"

"Much as I hate to admit it, yes."

She nodded and continued, "Then Phillip lies about the date he arrived in town and coincidently there was a stranger at the garage that day. Philip's angry about the wake, and Leroy is hurt. If Cinnamon hadn't alerted me, we might not have found him before he bled out. Which would make two murders. Then this receipt turns up. If these things aren't connected, then I'm a terrible baker."

His mouth twitched for barely a second. "So, when I asked you to leave this case to the department, you heard instead, 'Go ahead and solve the crime'?"

She flushed. "Not exactly. I just didn't agree with your take on things and had an inkling there was more to this case than gaining a garage. Someone in Fairview knows more than the rest of us, and I think we should pool resources to find out who."

He shook his head, and when Cinnamon scratched at the screen door, Walker took his coffee and crouched down to study the beagle. "Did you see something?"

"Woof." Cinnamon nodded her head.

"You saw who hurt Leroy?"

"Woof, woof!"

Walker stood and faced Lyra, his eyes twinkling. "I guess that settles it. Getting a confession might be a little trickier though."

"There's no need to ridicule me," she said through clenched teeth. "Cinnamon did see something that night, and if you won't do anything about this, then I will."

He stood and placed his mug on the counter with a bang. "I don't appreciate your threat, Lyra. I'm not making light of Rob's death, but I also don't want finding the person responsible to become your focus so much that you don't take care and end up hurt. Since you can't or won't listen to me, I'll say it again, stay out of police business, and this time it isn't a request."

"Or what? You'll arrest me?"

He shrugged. "If I have to."

Lyra flinched. His cool tone brought her back from the anger that threatened to overwhelm her. Not intending to rile him up this badly, she'd backed him into a corner, which meant he'd be unlikely to keep her updated in the future. "I do appreciate all you've done so far, and I apologize for going off that way. I guess it's all been too much for me."

He raised an eyebrow. "Okay, but did you hear what I said?"

"Yes, Sheriff."

"I'm just going to throw this out there—I don't trust you."

She blinked several times. "Charming."

"You know what I mean."

Lyra studied her hands. "All I do know is that this whole business with Rob and Leroy is upsetting, and it would be nice if you could cut me some slack and get off my case."

"That's just it," he growled. "You have no case. I'm the one with the job to do, and maybe if you thought about how upsetting it is for the rest of us who were friends of Rob's, you wouldn't go ahead and push all my buttons." Snatching the evidence and his hat from the table, Walker marched out the door.

Lyra's frustration threatened to boil over. For some reason, Walker drove her to say things best kept to herself. If only Kaden were here to offer his calming influence.

Having watched the interchange, Cinnamon paced outside the door, and Lyra hurried to comfort her. "I'm okay. The sheriff won't hurt me." In fact, he'd said that he didn't want her to get hurt. Which was an odd thing to say to someone you didn't like.

The beagle nodded her head, then came to her food bowl outside the door and sniffed again. All thoughts of Walker tuned to concern. Cinnamon's lack of appetite was strange. She hadn't lost any weight, but was sluggish and picky over what she did eat. A trip to the vet wasn't Cin's favorite thing to do, so Lyra was going to have to be sneaky about it.

22

Yawning after another restless night, Lyra stirred the soup and almost threw the spoon when Poppy burst through the kitchen door.

"He's here!"

Patricia wiped her hands on a cloth and put her hands on her shoulders. "Calm down, child. Who's here?"

"Mr. McKenna. He wants his book."

With false calm, Lyra put the lid back on the huge pot. "Leave this to me." Removing her apron, she walked casually into the diner, where Phillip waited at the counter. "I'm sorry, Mr. McKenna, we don't have your book."

"I left it right there." He pointed to the table in the corner. "I forgot it after your customers heckled me earlier. Someone must know where it is, unless one of your customers took it." He glowered at the room in general and was met with several glares right back at him.

The last thing Lyra needed was a war in the diner. "No need to accuse anybody of wrongdoing, Mr. McKenna. We did find it and handed it over to the police."

He frowned. "Why would you do that?"

"I suggest you talk to Sheriff Walker. He seemed quite interested in its contents."

"This is ridiculous; it's just an old book."

When Lyra offered nothing more, he marched out the door. The knitting group had watched the entire exchange, and Carrie-Ann gave Lyra a thumbs up.

Goodness knows she didn't like Phillip McKenna, but unless he was a brilliant actor, he'd just confirmed that he knew nothing about the receipt. This was good and made her feel like she was getting somewhere, even if it was simply crossing off suspects. She returned to her soup and gave it a thoughtful stir. There was still the matter of the herbs to tackle.

"Well? What did he say?" Patricia asked impatiently.

Lyra had forgotten they would be waiting for answers. She faced them and shrugged. "I'm convinced he had no idea what I was talking about."

"I don't know; he's good at pretending." Poppy pouted. "I'm glad he's gone, and I hope the sheriff does arrest him."

"But there was no benefit to him in planting it for us to find. Anyway, with him going to the station to get his book back, they'll have the conversation about the receipt, then the sheriff can make up his mind," Lyra reasoned, not sure if she was trying to convince herself or the others.

"Did he say something to make you believe he's innocent?" Poppy asked.

Lyra frowned. "It's what he didn't say."

"I don't understand."

"All I know is that I feel weird about being so convinced he's guilty of everything for so long, and now that this receipt turned up, I can't shake the doubt."

"He hasn't been very nice to us," Patricia reminded her.

Poppy nodded effusively. "And he wouldn't speak to his dad, who was the sweetest man."

"That is true, dear, but Like Sheriff Walker said, that's not a reason to condemn him just yet."

"I can't believe you're sticking up for that horrible man." Poppy threw up her hands. "What about Leroy? Have you forgotten about him?"

Patricia tutted. "No one could forget that, dear. Lyra has a process, and once she works through it all, she'll find out what happened."

Poppy nodded. "Sorry to get carried away. I just can't bear the thought of that man getting away with hurting Leroy. I better get back out front." She left the room as if she had the weight of the world on her shoulders.

"Poor thing; she's very fond of Leroy," Patricia said.

Lyra plated up the soup orders. "We all are, and I do want to find the person who attacked him and put all this behind us. The problem is I've been so bent on all these things being connected, I hadn't thought about each one separately. There are so many things that don't make sense that it feels like déjà vu."

"There were certainly a lot of things happening before you left LA that were confusing just like this case, but how can Rob, Leroy, and the break-in be separate? I mean, you're talking about three things happening in the space of a week."

"Exactly." Lyra shrugged. "What are the odds on that?"

"Slim, I'd say." Patricia pulled out a tray of small bread rolls from the oven and in their place slipped in trays of apple pies.

"That's what I thought," Lyra said aloud. What she didn't add was that it was still possible.

"Mom, I'm going to take Cinnamon to the V-E-T."

A scrabbling on the verandah made Lyra dash for the door. "Come back right now!" she yelled at the brown blur rushing through the hedge and not bothering with the gap.

A head popped out through the lower branches.

"Yes, I'm talking to you. Come." She almost laughed at the slumped shoulders and drooping head. Big eyes looked up sadly when the beagle got back to the veranda and slumped at her feet. "For goodness' sake, it's a little checkup, that's all."

Grabbing the lead from the coat rack just inside the door, Lyra clipped it on. She waved at Patricia through the window, and they went down the alley with Cinnamon behaving as if she were being led to the gallows.

Jessie the vet sweet-talked Cinnamon into a thorough examination and, after commenting on the beagle being a little heavy, reassured them both that it was only a minor gastric problem. With a careful watch on food intake, Cinnamon would be fine in a day or two.

Relieved at the prognosis, Lyra now knew that someone else was feeding Cinnamon. Obviously far too much and something that didn't agree with her.

She would speak to her staff, and if that didn't fix things, she'd have to put a sign up at the diner.

"This is going to be hard, Cinnamon, but you need to go on a diet."

The beagle's head dropped once more.

"If you'd be a little more discerning, this wouldn't be an issue," Lyra explained. A shiver ran down her back. Was this a coincidence, or could it be linked to the fact that someone had also tampered with Rob's food?

She had to find out about the herbs, and if she was right somehow talking the sheriff into believing her.

23

Leroy came to work on Tuesday, and Poppy all but threw herself into his arms. He grinned and awkwardly patted her back. "I'm fine."

"I'm so glad to see you." Her voice wobbled. "I thought you mightn't want to come back to work here."

"Why on earth not?"

Her mouth dropped open. "Because you got hurt, of course."

"If we stopped doing things because we got hurt, we'd be stuck at home twiddling our thumbs."

Lyra agreed with his take on things, but Poppy wasn't so sure.

"You're not mad about what happened?"

"I wouldn't say that, but you can't dwell on what might happen or even what did. That way the bad guy is the only winner. Besides, people like that always put a foot wrong eventually, and then the police will catch them."

"But what kind of person would do that?" asked Earl.

"That's easy, son—bullies, cowards, and the greedy."

Judging by the frowns and level of concentration, it

seemed that her staff was trying to picture who might fit into each category, and Lyra decided they needed to move on. "We're glad to have you back, but are you absolutely sure it's not too early?"

Leroy grabbed his apron and tied it behind him with a flourish. "I had an appointment with my doctor this morning, and he agrees it was a mild concussion. As long as I don't overdo it, I'm good to go."

"You're a very lucky man, and I'll be watching that you don't," Patricia told him as she sliced up salad ingredients.

"Yes, ma'am. I thought I'd do reduced hours today and be back on board tomorrow at the right time."

"You start and finish when you feel like it," Lyra told him.

He grinned, and within a few minutes, it was as if he had never been away.

Dan stopped by for breakfast and, after greeting Leroy, sat at Maggie's table.

She raised an eyebrow when he simply stared. "What's up?"

"I could ask you the same question," he leaned back and crossed his ankles.

"You'll have to give me a clue."

"A few people dropped by the garage yesterday afternoon to book in their cars, including Poppy's mom, who drives a very nice Porsche."

"I guess that's why we didn't see you last night. Although, I can't think what it has to do with me."

"As it happens, I did get started on one of the cars left in the garage that have been waiting the longest, but that's not it. A couple of customers asked after my wife and kids. Apparently, they're around here somewhere. Could you point me in the right direction? It appears I've misplaced them."

Maggie stiffened, her face a bright red. "I don't know what you're talking about."

"That's odd." He scratched his head. "I have it on good authority that this information came from you."

"Oh, I remember now." She waved her hand in the air. "It was a joke. Some of the knitting ladies were trying to fix you up with their daughters, and I knew you'd hate that."

"I see. So, you were just doing me a favor by spreading lies about me."

"I wouldn't put it quite like that. Besides, you should thank me for thinking on my feet, so they'd leave you alone."

He roared with laughter. "Why, thank you, Maggie. I appreciate how much you care for my welfare. I hope I can return the favor very soon."

She flushed again and looked down at her laptop. "Go away. I'm busy."

"Yes, ma'am. Will I see you later for some more tutorials on running my business?"

"If I have time."

He waited for her to look at him, then winked. "I'm pretty sure you do."

Lyra and Leroy shared smirks. These two were so funny. Did they really think they were fooling anyone? It was obvious, and getting more so every day, that they were attracted to each other. Maggie spent a lot of time with Dan at the garage, and always came home a little giggly and just before him. They also made sure to arrive at the diner at different times, but Lyra and Patricia were under no illusion that bookwork was barely a fraction of their incentive to be together.

Leroy began to whistle, and Lyra decided to put on the mixer for her muffins. Maggie wouldn't take kindly to her laughing at his rendition of "Love Is a Many-Splendored Thing."

In such a short time, the world around her had returned to a new normal. Maggie worked at the kitchen table. Leroy and Patricia cooked together as if that had always been the way. Earl kept the place spotless and would go back to his usual hours of starting and ending later, which ensured the kitchen was clean for the next day. Poppy was busy taking orders, serving at the counter, and avoiding her mom. And Cinnamon had been given a clean bill of health, except for a considerable weight gain.

Lyra could only assume that customers had been feeding her out on the verandah when she wasn't looking, because the beagle's diet was strictly monitored.

Once the muffins were in the oven and pies stood on the counter cooling, Lyra joined Maggie to tackle the diner's paperwork, which had been neglected for a few days.

"It's good to have Leroy back." Maggie nodded at the cook, who shared a joke with Patricia.

Lyra nodded. "It's a relief to see him doing so well."

They watched him pace around the place doing inventory, when he suddenly began making weird sounds.

Lyra put the lid down on her laptop. "Is there a problem, Leroy?

He looked up from the clipboard he carried and frowned. "We need several things that are getting low, but I'm wondering how much steak you got through while I was off work?"

"I'd say about the usual amount. Why do you ask?"

"We're almost out, and the next delivery is not due until Friday."

"It's strange that I didn't notice."

"I better get a delivery ASAP, but this doesn't look good."

Lyra's stomach dipped. "Are you saying that someone's been helping themselves?"

"It sure looks like it, but who would do that? As per your

instructions, I let anyone who works here buy whatever we sell at cost, and they can have a meal every day, so there's no need to steal."

Maggie pursed her lips. "Having no need doesn't always stop people from taking what they shouldn't."

Lyra shook her head. "I can't believe anyone working for me would take steak in those amounts."

"What if they were selling it?" Maggie asked.

Lyra flinched, hating the idea that one of her staff would do that. "You, Mom, and Dan eat with me. Leroy was in the hospital, then recuperating. That leaves Earl and Poppy. Neither are here alone, and the place is never empty except for when it's closed."

"When you say it like that, it does seem a stretch too far," Leroy said, but the frown stayed.

Unfortunately, the seed was well and truly sown. Steak didn't just walk out the door, and Lyra's mind ticked over several scenarios. What if this was a completely separate issue?

Maggie tilted her head. "You look like you've thought of something,"

Lyra turned to Leroy. "What if the night you were attacked, it was because an opportunistic thief came to rob the place? They might have hidden in the bathroom and not realized that when everyone else left you were still here."

"So, they were trying to get out and had to get past me first," he suggested.

"Exactly. There was no money left on site because we weren't open for sales. They probably knew that and thought they could take something to sell. It would also need to be something small enough to carry, which would discount any of the industrial equipment."

"You would have noticed that kind of thing missing," Maggie added. "All they could take was food."

"If that's really what happened, who do we know so desperate for money that wouldn't raise suspicions being at the wake?" Lyra asked.

"You mean a local?" Leroy leaned against the counter. "There are plenty of people feeling the pinch, but none who spring to mind that desperate."

Patricia gasped. "Unless the intention is to put the blame for everything that's happened elsewhere."

"Like Phillip McKenna," Maggie suggested.

"I don't see how he could, Mags. Everyone knows by now who he is and what he looks like, and that he didn't want to be associated with this wake." Lyra paced between the table and the counter. "If he was anywhere near the place, someone would have said something by now."

"This is doing my head in," Maggie groaned.

Leroy rubbed his temples. "And mine."

Lyra was immediately concerned for him. "Let's not dwell on this right now. I'll speak to the sheriff. He could spread the word that there might be black-market meat being sold in Fairview and possibly in neighboring towns."

The others got her pointed look and let the matter drop. Poor Leroy had been through enough, and it wasn't worth distressing him over the price of some steak.

24

Lyra answered the phone, careful not to drip the lemon cream-cheese frosting off the spatula she held over a carrot cake.

"It's Sheriff Walker. I got your message. I'll be there in half an hour."

Without waiting for her reply, he hung up. Lyra glanced at the clock. At least it was better he'd be here before the lunch rush. Only, now she had half an hour to dwell on what to say. By his tone, he wasn't in the mood for discussion.

Actually, there was little time to dwell on anything. Patricia scooped dough out of the industrial mixer to knead into pastry. Leroy was making pie filling, and Lyra had to finish icing the cake and then put a lasagna together.

"Poppy, Earl, the sheriff is coming to see me soon. While I'm speaking to him, please help Leroy if we get busy."

Earl nodded eagerly. "I could clean tables if that would help you, Poppy."

"Thanks, that will free me up to serve." Poppy fussed with a display of fresh cupcakes. "Do you know what he wants, Lyra?"

She hadn't mentioned the missing steak, because she wanted to discuss things with Walker first. "I'm not sure, but hopefully it won't take long, and we'll be done by lunchtime."

"He's here quite a lot these days."

Lyra couldn't deny it, or that she didn't mind as much as she used to. "Sheriff Walker's been visiting all the businesses in town trying to lock down everyone's whereabouts during the crimes."

"Is he having any luck?" Earl asked. "Everyone says how long it's taking and that they don't like the thought of a cold-blooded killer out there."

Patricia tutted. "Maybe that's why he's stopping by. We could do with good news, and then we can stop worrying about it."

"I wish everything could go back to how it was." Poppy's voice hitched, and she hurried out with the cupcakes.

"The poor girl is terribly stressed," Leroy noted sympathetically.

Patricia nodded. "She does look peaky."

"Maybe I've been asking too much of her after what's happened," Lyra said. "It's hard for all of us to digest, but she's taken it all to heart."

"Although she was upset about Mr. McKenna dying, Leroy being hurt affected her the most." Earl blushed and bent over the dishwasher.

"Plus, she has you-know-who for a mother," Maggie muttered.

"Shush," Lyra warned.

"It just slipped out." Maggie glanced around her. "Besides, Poppy's in the diner."

"That's not the point. If she was in earshot and you let something like that slip, how would you feel?"

Her friend reddened. "You're right. I do feel sorry for her and don't want to upset her any more than she already is. It's just that I heard the two of them arguing, and Vanessa was being downright mean about Poppy going back to school."

"I hadn't realized it was getting worse." Lyra sighed at the admission. It seemed that life was hard for everyone at the moment, and she decided right then to do something to cheer them up. It would need to be something appropriate, that wouldn't give the impression they were making light about anything that had happened.

She was still mulling this over when Walker arrived via the veranda entrance, and right behind him was someone she was far more delighted to see.

"Kaden! What on earth are you doing here?" She ran into his arms, and he laughed while Cinnamon turned circles and barked at the door.

"Now that's what I call a welcome. Cinnamon saw me arrive and led me straight to you."

"This is a lovely surprise," Patricia called from the grill. "How are you?"

"Wonderful, especially now I've seen that Lyra is okay. I hope it's not a bad time, but I decided to take a few hours off."

A cough from behind them turned out to be a stony-faced Walker. "Sorry to interrupt, Lyra, but I need to speak with you."

Kaden kept his arm around her shoulder, which somehow made things a little awkward.

"Of course. This my good friend Kaden Hunter from Portland. Kaden, meet Sheriff Walker."

Eyeing each other up and down, the men shook hands.

"If this is official business, would you like me to wait outside?" Kaden offered.

"If you wouldn't mind," Walker dismissed him.

Lyra held onto Kaden's arm. "He knows of our problems, so I'd like him to stay."

Walker grunted once and nodded across the kitchen. "Good to see you back in action, Leroy."

"Thanks, Sheriff. Any leads as to who attacked me?"

"Not at this stage. We did a test on the skillet, which proved it was the weapon, but there were no fingerprints. It could be they wore gloves or that the food wiped any prints off by the time we got to it. We're still on the case though." He turned back to Lyra. "I've spoken to Mr. McKenna and am satisfied with his account of things. Now, this meat business, you're quite convinced it's a theft issue?"

"I wouldn't have called you unless I was sure. Why do you sound like you don't believe me?" She noted the difference in tone between talking to Leroy and then her. She also didn't like the way he glossed over Phillip and the receipts, but there were a lot of people here and perhaps he didn't want to share the information with everyone.

"It's not that." He shuffled his feet.

She crossed her arms. "What is it then?"

"Missing meat doesn't seem to fit in with everything else going on. I just wanted to make sure that it isn't a book-keeping error or something like that."

"With three sets of eyes on the accounts, it isn't likely to be a bookkeeping issue, and as I pointed out, there is a connection."

He raised an eyebrow. "You mentioned that Phillip McKenna eats steak here every day. That's hardly a crime when I'm pretty sure many other customers have the same tastes."

"Even if it wasn't him, we buy the same amount, give or take a little, every week. Just a few days after the last order was delivered, it was nearly all gone."

"Perhaps you had better sales than you anticipated."

Lyra strode to the corner she used as an office and brought him the folder with the daily printouts of orders. "I copied the week's sales for you. I think it's very easy to see that there were nowhere near the sales to account for all the meat Leroy ordered."

He took them and flicked through the papers. She'd highlighted each steak sale so he couldn't miss them, yet he frowned.

"This is interesting, but I don't know how much steak you had."

Lyra handed him another piece of paper which was the invoice for the last order.

"There does appear to be a large discrepancy," he eventually admitted.

"Maybe he just wanted to annoy me." Lyra blanched as she heard how lame that sounded. "Okay, let's say it wasn't Phillip McKenna; you have to admit that somebody had to have stolen the meat."

"I'll file a report," he said grudgingly. "But you have to appreciate that it's right down the list for us at the moment."

She nodded. "I realize that it should be, *if* it had nothing to do with the murder and Leroy being attacked."

His fingers raked his hair, then he pulled out a notebook. Scribbling a few lines, he tapped the paper. "Go ahead and tell me who has access to the diner apart from you, and of course Leroy."

"Mom, Maggie, and Dan. That's it."

"What about Poppy and Earl?"

"They don't have keys, as they only work when some or all of us are here."

"I've never seen him behind the counter, so why does Dan have keys?"

She huffed because he knew very well what Dan did for her. "He outfitted the diner and kitchen after he gutted it, and still does all the maintenance."

"And no one else can get in—like a supplier?"

189

"No. All deliveries are done when we're here and mostly in the early morning."

"Well, I guess that's it for now." He tucked the notebook back in his shirt pocket. "I'll let you know if I hear anything about any of the cases."

When he'd gone, Kaden leaned against the counter. "Wow. He wasn't exactly enthusiastic."

"You're telling me. I do seem to have an unfortunate effect on police no matter where I am."

A hand on his chin, Kaden's eyes twinkled. "Sheesh, I can't think why."

He could always make her smile. "So now you know everything, what do you think?"

The answering smile slipped from his face. "I think you're in way over your head."

"Nothing new there." Patricia came and gave Kaden a belated hug. "So, what are you really doing here?"

He snorted. "Like I said, I needed to check if Lyra was really okay and to see if I can help in any way."

"There must be something?"

Lyra shrugged. "I need to find out who killed Rob and hurt Leroy. The steak, I don't care so much about, I'm just worried that it's a huge clue that fits somewhere."

"Here we go again," Maggie muttered.

"That's not helpful, Mags."

"Neither is you putting a giant target on your back."

Kaden nodded. "I have to agree."

"I haven't even told you my plan yet," Lyra said reasonably.

"You actually have one?" Maggie scoffed.

"I do, it's just not fully formed."

"Go on," Kaden encouraged.

"We buy more steak to tempt the thief."

He frowned. "If it's a person you know, don't you think that will be a little obvious?"

Aware that it wasn't exactly a gold nugget, Lyra was disappointed by his reaction. "Maybe. What do you suggest?"

"If someone is stealing from you, then there's probably more than steak finding its way out the door. It might be a good idea to prioritize an audit of all your inventory."

Lyra chewed her lip for a second. "I was planning on doing one after we close today.."

Kaden removed his denim jacket. "Shall we get started?"

"You mean now?" Lyra protested. "But you've come for a visit."

"We can visit and still look through files. It will be like old times and seems to me that an extra pair of hands wouldn't go astray."

His grin was infectious. "Thanks, that would be wonderful. If you're sure you don't mind?"

"You'd do the same for me. In fact, I believe you already did."

She laughed and helped the smirking Maggie clear the table.

"Kaden, why don't you and Mags start with last week's file while I print off more from before that. I assume we'll be focusing on big ticket items, like other meat or expensive ingredients?"

"Yes. While we'll check everything like you normally do, it wouldn't make sense for a thief to take anything too cheap or bulky like flour. They'd still have to get it off the premises without anyone noticing."

As Lyra went to the corner, she passed by the cooler. It was the major thoroughfare out to the veranda. Anyone going in and out of there could be seen by people working in the kitchen. The same was true of the walk-in pantry on the same wall. Anyone wanting to steal from either of these places would have to be superfast and be sure that no one was in the kitchen or entering it. That would be rare and not something a stranger could pinpoint with any accuracy, as breaks were taken when the diner was quiet and not at a particular time.

Maggie provided highlighters, and they sat at the table while Leroy and Patricia manned the kitchen. Poppy and Earl came in and out as usual, looking curious, but they didn't interrupt them.

Kaden tapped his papers. "I can't see any huge anomalies, although takings look to be down."

"Some of it is attributable to the wake. I closed the diner that afternoon and also donated all the food."

"That would explain one week. Before and after look off as well."

She leaned over his shoulder. "Hmm. You're right. Shall we get started on the inventory in the chiller?"

Lyra collected Leroy's clipboard and checked what he had written down to purchase. Lyra tapped the paper. "Let's check these shelves."

They walked along the meat trays, which Kaden and Maggie counted, then called out amounts. Having already checked out what should be there, it was clear that numbers were lighter on everything, but mainly the steak.

Lyra kept her cool until they were done, and they moved into the pantry. "You know, there are definitely gaps here and there, which makes me think this has been going on a while."

Maggie nodded. "Whoever is helping themselves might be taking a little at a time so you don't notice."

She sucked in a breath. "Which means they must have a key. I feel sick about this."

"I know how that feels. First thing to do is to get Dan to change all the locks."

Kaden's sympathy was nearly her undoing, and she clenched her hand for a moment or two.

"He's so busy with the garage."

"Then get someone else. This is too important to leave."

She straightened her shoulders. "You're right. If Dan can't do it, he'll likely to know someone local who can."

"How about we take a break, and you show me around properly? I'd also like to see your house before I go."

"What an awful visit for your first time in Fairview."

"It's not all bad. Seeing and working with you would be perfect if it wasn't for the reason behind it."

She shook her head in wonder. "I am so glad you came."

Arm in arm, they walked around the kitchen and diner, and Lyra introduced Kaden to her customers. The knitting group were beside themselves with questions, which he answered good-naturedly. Eventually, Lyra had to cut them off by saying he had to leave soon.

"Come say goodbye before you leave," Patricia called to him as they escaped out the door.

"I will, and say hi to Dan."

They strolled to the farmhouse, laughing about his popularity with the ladies, and Lyra enjoyed showing off the remodeling.

"Wow, both places are great, and from what you've described as changes, Dan's done an awful lot."

"He's been awesome, and I couldn't have managed without him. That's why I think getting the garage is so good for him. This will be his own purpose and not mine."

"I'd go see him if I had time, but I'll be sure to come back very soon. Don't forget about changing the locks, call when you have any news at all, and promise me you'll be careful."

"I promise." She buried her face in his hard chest and soaked up the comfort found there.

25

That night Lyra and Patricia were going over the layout for the new cookbook. It was coming together nicely and wasn't too far off from being ready for her editor.

Patricia nudged her shoulder. "It was so kind of Kaden to come help you out today. I loved seeing the two of you together. It reminded me of those years watching you side by side, poring over cookbooks and challenging each other to do better. At first, I worried about the way he relentlessly pushed you. Then I saw how you rose to the challenge and blossomed. The fire in you both showed me you are kindred spirits."

Lyra smiled. "I don't know about the whole kindred spirits thing, but it does feel very natural to have him around, even though we haven't seen each other except on our phones for months."

"That's what real friendship is all about. When I saw Martha again, it was truly as if I'd come home in a more complete way than simply moving back in here." She nodded at the room around her.

It was natural that Mom had missed her friends, and

Lyra's guilt meter swung into action. She hadn't been as sympathetic as she should have—being busy was no excuse. Born and raised in Fairview, Patricia moved into this house as a newlywed, selling it without hesitation and leaving the only life she knew to be near her only child. Now Lyra owned it, and the place had changed significantly, yet somehow, she felt the same about it being home once more. It was more than the house or the town. It was being happy doing what they loved in a place that made her heart warm while being surrounded by good people. Mostly.

Breaking the reverie, Dan and Maggie returned from the garage with more books and a long wooden drawer.

"What have you got there?" Lyra asked.

"Rob's customer lists and his diary," Dan explained. "Sheriff Walker dropped them back to me today."

"His bookwork is impeccable." Maggie held one of them out to her. "Considering he did everything without the aid of a computer, it's amazing."

"I can't imagine working that way."

Patricia laughed. "You all have no idea. That's just how it was back then. I guess Rob saw no reason to change something that worked." She took the diary from Dan. "He always worked long hours, but after his wife died and his son left, he spent all his time at the garage."

Lyra touched the book reverently. "You can see the evidence written up in his careful handwriting. He booked at least three or four cars in every day. Plus, he often had cash jobs from walk-ins."

Dan nodded. "His business was still booming when he passed away. I'm a little nervous that I won't do it justice."

"What you don't know about cars hasn't been written," Maggie told him.

He reddened and placed the wooden drawer on the coffee

table in front of Lyra. "Look at the cards. Rob had a rapport with every customer."

Lyra flicked through the first couple of rectangular cards filling the drawer. In alphabetical order they showed the name, address, phone number, and details of each car's owner. Underneath this was a line of dates and what each service or repair consisted of. "I see what you mean; this is so precise."

"It must help that he knew most people, and now you'll get to know them too," Maggie insisted. "You're personable enough."

Dan gave a wry grin. "Thanks for the vote of confidence. I do need to put things in motion pretty soon, otherwise they'll be going elsewhere."

Patricia tutted. "I'm sure that won't be the case. People are understanding enough to give you a little leeway and not harass you to fix the cars that were booked in."

"Actually, I have had a few more inquiries. I asked them to call back in a couple of days. My aim is to get the ball rolling by Monday."

"Good for you." Lyra loved seeing his excitement, even if it was tempered with apprehension. "Once you get into it, you'll be fine."

"I hope so. Maggie's helped a lot with setting up new accounts, and I've familiarized myself with the garage. I plan on getting the last two bedrooms at the farmhouse finished this weekend. By the way, there's a couple of rooms above the garage, so I'm going to move in there."

He said this so casually, yet Lyra's stomach dropped. With no way of knowing if the person responsible for all the terrible things happening was still around or not, having him move out made her uneasy. "Is the space habitable?"

Maggie crinkled her nose. "Personally, I wouldn't stay

there. Most of it has been a dumping ground for spare parts, and it's musty and dank."

Dan frowned at her before turning to Lyra. "It's not so bad. I'll do it up when I have the time. Besides, you need your home back."

"We're doing fine just the way we are. Please don't let that be a reason to rush into anything. We love having you around, don't we, Maggie?"

"Sure." Maggie flicked one of the papers she pretended to read.

"Why not stay until you've fixed it up?" Even to Lyra it sounded pleading. "Only if you want to."

He looked between the two women, then shrugged. "Thanks, Lyra. Maybe it would be best to stay with you for a little longer. I'm not sure how much free time I'll have to work on the rooms over the garage once I start full-time there."

Deep down she knew he had to move on. Living with three women was undoubtedly no picnic, but it would be hard not to have Dan's talents available when required. And even harder not to have his upbeat personality around.

Somehow reading her mind, he looked her squarely in the eyes. "It's not like I'm moving far. If you need me, for anything, don't hesitate to ask. You never have to worry about me not wanting to help out."

Her eyes misted. "Thank you, Dan. You have no idea how much better that makes me feel, and I promise I'll try not to be a pain."

"Don't talk crazy. Besides, you'll always need a taster, right?"

She sniffed. "Always. And you better come for meals."

"Seriously?" Maggie hiccupped. "The man can't cook. You won't be able to get rid of him."

"I, for one, don't intend to try." Patricia had a distinct quiver in her voice.

It looked as though Lyra wasn't the only one who would miss having Dan around the house.

They spent the rest of the evening piecing together the last week of Rob's life through his diary and receipt books. This wasn't as miserable as it sounded, due to what Rob wrote about each customer. He must have known each of them well, because he included notes about their families and pets. Except for that manufactured receipt, and the one two days earlier, everything seemed to be business as usual.

Lyra flicked back to the diary several times. Somehow, she had to find a way to match the handwriting. The problem was most things were done electronically or people paid by cash. This was the first time she'd felt annoyed about checks not being in use the way they used to be.

26

All morning, Lyra wanted to get the diary and her conjecture to the sheriff, but they were swamped. Poppy should have been out with the customers. Instead, she stood at the sink getting in Earl's way.

"I need you out front; the diner's full," Lyra pointed out as she filled a tray for the display case with individual cherry pies.

Poppy gulped. "I just need a minute."

Knowing she was still suffering, Lyra wanted to be patient, but her customers weren't as sympathetic.

Maggie jumped up immediately. "I'll help clear tables."

Grateful, Lyra followed her out. The knitting club ladies looked to be the most antsy about the poor service, so Lyra headed their way first.

"About time," Vanessa narrowed her eyes at the internal doorway. "Where's Poppy?"

Lyra tapped her tablet. "She's on her break. What can I get you?"

Vanessa muttered something about easy work while the others placed their orders.

"I'll have the eggs Benedict and a latte," Carrie-Ann said.

"Did you want something, Vanessa?"

"I'll have the soup."

No please or thank you followed, so Lyra headed back to the kitchen and looked around for Poppy, but the girl had disappeared.

Leroy waved her over to the grill. "I sent her to get a couple of things from the store."

Lyra nodded. "She wasn't doing much good here, and I'm sure the fresh air will do her some good."

"That's what I thought. Sorry if I overstepped. I know you're swamped out there."

"Don't worry about that, and thanks for supporting her. She hasn't said much to me, and I can't seem to get through to her, so I'm glad she has you."

Was that a blush she saw?

He waved her away. "Earl's keeping an eye on her too."

The boy nodded. "Yeah, she's real sad all the time, but she won't talk about it."

Lyra took the hint and let him be. It was enough to know that her team cared about each other. Although, it was a shame, Poppy's mom was so hard on her. Still, there was little she could do about that, and she had work to do. Lifting a tray of loaded wedges, she headed back to her customers.

Maggie was filling coffee without being asked, and between the two of them and Earl, they quickly cleared the backlog of dishes and customers, as well as serving the meals and drinks.

Almost simultaneously, the knitting club left, and Poppy arrived back. She couldn't meet Lyra's eyes, but she put on her apron and wiped down the nearest table.

Lyra motioned for Maggie to follow her into the kitchen. "Do you think she'll be okay? I don't know what to do for her," she whispered when they were out of earshot.

"You do plenty. She'd deal with everything a lot better if her mom would stay off her case."

"What's Vanessa got to do with Poppy being so upset?"

"She's hounding the girl to get back to studying, and Poppy doesn't want to."

"Did she tell you this?"

"I heard her talking to Leroy. He was really good about it and encouraged her to do what she wants. As far as I'm concerned, he said all the right things."

"That's good, but her mom won't appreciate him interfering."

"Not at all. In fact, she's been more unpleasant than usual, so I imagine she knows we won't dissuade Poppy from staying. It must be awful to go home to an argument every night."

Lyra grimaced. "Speaking of unpleasant, I haven't seen Arabelle lately, have you?"

"Not for a while. I heard Vanessa talking about her. Seems there is more bad blood than we knew about between those two."

"I wonder what that's about."

"You'll never get anything out of them."

"Mmmm. But I know who might like to tell me what they know."

Maggie frowned, then her eyes lit up. "Carrie-Ann."

"She loves gossip and would welcome the idea that she's helping by sharing it."

They laughed quietly but stopped when Poppy came to collect an order. She didn't seem to notice and kept her head down as if she didn't want to engage with any of them. However, Earl wasn't as good at reading body language.

"Hey, Poppy. Want to have lunch together?"

"No, thanks."

She grabbed an order of burger and fries and hurried out, leaving Earl looking like a kicked puppy.

Lyra took him a dirty pan. "You've done nothing wrong. Poppy's just having a hard time at the moment."

He nodded, still looking upset. "I just want to make her feel better."

"I know, but pushing her won't help right now. We just need a little patience while she figures things out for herself."

"Okay. I'll leave her be."

Earl didn't look convinced, and Lyra sighed. She hardly fit the criteria to be an agony aunt. Hopefully Carrie-Ann would shed some light on Poppy's issue, and they could all help the young woman.

At this rate she wouldn't get to the sheriff's office until after lunch.

Fortunately, Dan arrived with a smile and his toolbox. "I managed to get a new set of keys and spares, so I thought I'd come by and change them now, if that suits you."

"Great. Can you do the shop first, then back here?"

"You bet."

He could be heard greeting everyone, and there were no complaints about the noise as he changed the lock, which meant the knitting club hadn't arrived yet.

It didn't take too long, and having one thing sorted lifted her spirits. Dan hung around for coffee and pie with Maggie. It was bittersweet to hear them making plans for Dan's new apartment, so she left for the sheriff's office.

27

"This is important." Lyra waved the diary at Officer Moore. "The sheriff will want to see this evidence, and I'm not letting it out of my sight." She added that when Janie made to grab it.

"Let her in." Walker's voice boomed through the open door.

Lyra had never been in his office. Files were stacked in piles on his desk, and he looked up from one relatively thick one, then firmly closed it.

"I trust you do actually have something for me."

She dropped the diary on his desk, making the nearest stack wobble. Fortunately, it didn't collapse, and she let out a breath. "Dan's been going through the customer list for the next few months. Every person who was due a service is in here, and the reminders were all manually done, and often verbally as well, which he made note of. He did send out letters to those living out of town."

"I saw this the day we went through the garage. Did you find something new?"

"Rob also made a note of registration numbers, which

match the ones found in the receipt book. His accounting was meticulous. There was no money received on the day of the false receipt. Only on the day that Phillip actually got his car repaired. He wasn't here the day Rob died after all."

"I know. He had an alibi for that day. There was no chance he was at the house or the garage on the day Rob was killed."

Lyra gasped. "Why didn't you tell me?"

Walker ran his fingers through his hair. "I don't have to tell you anything. Plus, I told you not to interfere. More than once."

She shook her head, unable to let this go. "If you know for sure it wasn't Phillip, then who else are you checking on? Surely you are still trying to solve this case."

"If I thought you were serious, I'd be insulted. I can assure you that there are several officers checking our leads. Before you ask, nothing we've found will be shared until we can use the information in the best way possible."

Lyra sighed. "Let me get this straight. You do think there is something else going on, but you're worried that if I know what it is, I'll shoot my mouth off."

His mouth twitched. "I wouldn't have put it so bluntly."

"What if I promised not to?"

"Even if you weren't some famous chef, thinking she deserves privileges over everyone else, you do tell your friends everything."

There wasn't much she could say to that. She didn't deserve preferential treatment, and living and working with Dan, Maggie, and Mom meant there was a lot of time for talking after the day was done. "I can keep a secret if I need to," she added half-heartedly.

He raised an eyebrow. "The only ones I see you keeping are from me."

"That isn't my intention. You never took me seriously, so I felt I couldn't tell you everything."

"And there lies the problem. Picking and choosing what you tell me shouldn't be a consideration, because I'm the sheriff."

"I realize that. Only, in the beginning, I thought you didn't care about the town. If you remember, you were pretty sour towards me when I arrived."

He stacked a couple of files together, tapping them noisily on the desk to straighten them. "I wanted to keep an open mind, but it seemed to me that you were bringing all your big-town troubles with you. Troubles we could do without when we had enough of our own. Like fighting off the developers, who are regrouping as we speak."

That gave her pause. "Are they really?"

"That's a conversation for another day."

"Fine, but you also thought I was somehow cashing in on my fame."

"The thought did cross my mind," he said sheepishly.

"Then you'll be pleased to note that I am not rolling in cash. After my ex-agent backstabbed me and I lost my shows, my accountant cleaned me out. Things were so bad I had to sell my amazing restaurant and apartment. I spent all my savings buying the diner and the farmhouse, as well as getting the diner up and running and the house somewhat livable. The diner is doing great and paying its way, but it's no gold mine. My fame is what's kept me afloat by way of royalties from the shows and my cookbooks." She blinked a few times, unsure why she'd just told him all this. "By the way, you're the only one in town I've said any of that to."

Walker hung on every word. "I see. You're trusting me to keep that quiet in return for me telling you about Rob's death?"

Lyra chewed her bottom lip for a moment. "That wasn't

the reason, but the fact is, I wouldn't be averse to hearing the truth."

He scratched his head. "This doesn't go out of this room."

She nodded seriously.

"Rob did die of a heart attack—after he'd been drugged. He was given a concoction of two herbs that together affected the medication he was on, basically nullifying it."

Lyra couldn't pretend to be surprised, but the confirmation heightened her anger at the murderer.

"The biggest clue, and one I haven't shared with anyone other than my superiors, is that we know someone tried to give him CPR. While we did manage a DNA sample, we can't get a hit on the national database. This implies, along with the absence of forced entry, that it wasn't a known criminal —but a person known to Rob. The problem is that there are a dozen fingerprints in the house, and naturally, other than Rob's, Dan's are everywhere."

It took a little time for all this to sink in, even though she had already accepted that the killer was a local. "Well, of course there would be plenty of Dan's fingerprints around the house. He lived there for months and was doing some renovations."

"I understand that, but like I say, it doesn't make things any easier."

She nodded. "That's why you interrogated Dan more so than anyone else. Were there prints that surprised you?"

He sighed. "Yes. People who I didn't imagine would visit him at home."

"People like...?"

"Let's just say people who gave the impression that they weren't fond of Rob."

Walker was clearly not going to reveal the suspects, and Lyra could understand that. Besides, she had a fair idea who he was referring to. Arabelle came to mind. Those two had no love lost between them. Or so they'd made out.

"I can see the wheels turning, and I don't want you going around town chasing anyone down."

"I wouldn't dream of it."

"Yes, you would. And that could have a detrimental effect on this case."

"I don't want that to happen. I guess you have a plan, which is why you haven't said more about Rob's death."

Walker nodded. "My intention is to flush out whoever killed him."

"But he's dead, so why would they come forward now?"

"They won't want to, but something drove them to such a desperate act. Whatever that is, it can't be resolved yet."

She grimaced. "Money. It's always about money."

"It often is, but not as much as you'd think."

She gasped. "You know who it is."

"I'm not certain, but I have a suspect in mind."

Lyra wanted to ask if it was Arabelle. It was literally on the tip of her tongue, but by the set of his mouth, she'd already pressed the sheriff as far as she thought he'd go. "Thank you for telling me the truth. Knowing that you are doing something to find the killer does help."

"Since I'm merely doing my job, I won't say you're welcome, but I do know how you feel. Rob was a good man, and he deserves to rest easy." The terseness slipped away, and he ended the sentence with genuine sadness.

This was the first time she'd seen how truly affected he was by Rob's death. Lyra gulped. "The fact that the killer tried CPR means that they had some remorse, only it was too late."

"Unfortunately, I think that's exactly what happened."

Lyra suddenly had an idea. "What if I could get you that DNA?"

"Good grief, woman! Did you listen at all to me saying to stay out of this investigation?"

"I did. It's just that if you have no clear reason to get a warrant for your suspect, then what better way than from the diner. Most people come in at least once a week. It would be relatively easy to get a sample."

He grasped her shoulder and escorted her to the door as if he couldn't wait to get rid of her. "That's not how it works. There are far too many issues with having DNA admissible in a trial. For one thing the sample has to come from a reputed source and be uncontaminated."

"So now, I'm contaminated and not reputable?"

"I don't think you're either of those things, but what I think doesn't matter."

He still had hold of her arm as they stared at each other. She hadn't noticed before how the gray in his eyes was flecked with blue, and suddenly the one thing she did know was that it mattered a great deal what he thought of her. "What about fingerprints?"

Suddenly he grinned, which lit up his whole face, and the small lines creasing around his eyes made him appear softer. Lyra was proud that she'd been the one to make that happen and hoped it wasn't a one-off.

"I'm not sure how they'll help at this stage because of how many people were in each place of interest. But I know you have access to some of the suspects, and it could help me narrow things down without the need to use them in evidence." His fingers dug in a little more. Not enough to hurt, but she felt the warning. "There are a couple of rules if you're going to do this."

She didn't expect anything less.

"First, you will not mention this to anyone else. No one at all," he emphasized.

Lyra nodded.

"You take the glass or mug they use and wrap it in a cloth and call me or bring it here right away."

"I can do that."

"If anyone asks what you're doing, you'll have to lie."

That could be trickier, but Lyra was determined to make this happen, and nodded. "Whatever it takes."

"I don't like having you involved, but I'm going to show you a list. You cannot take it or write the names anywhere."

They walked back to his desk, and watching her intently, he pulled a piece of paper from a file.

She scanned it carefully, memorizing each name while trying to appear unfazed by what she read. "Okay, I've got them locked in."

He walked her to the door again. "Get the samples when you can, and keep me informed, but above all else, make sure you stay safe."

"I will," Lyra assured them both. As excited as she was to be doing something proactive, there were prickles of fear, which she decided was probably a good thing. It would stop her taking silly chances and help to keep her people safe.

Solving the case wouldn't bring Rob back, but the person who did this would never hurt anyone else.

28

On her return, the diner was relatively quiet, and as Lyra glanced around at her customers and prospective suspects, she was on edge. Why hadn't she asked Walker who she should target first? Did he think they were on the same page, so there was no need? Absolutely anyone could have been in Rob's house the day he died. Except it wasn't just anyone. It was someone who bore a grudge of such proportions that they'd done something they instantly regretted. At least that's how it played out in Lyra's mind, as well as the sheriff's, which made it more likely.

The knitting club chatted at a few decibels above everyone else, but for once they weren't talking about Rob. People couldn't mourn forever, but he'd only been buried a few days ago, and yet it looked as though life was back to normal for some. Which was far from the case for Lyra.

With Rob not coming in for a chat or meeting up for their regular walks, plus Arabelle not arriving at the same time every day since he died, things were very different. Lyra paused as she loaded pies into the display case. Why would Arabelle suddenly stop coming if she didn't care about Rob? Surely, she hadn't made the coffee and friand a habit just to annoy him. "Poppy, have you seen Arabelle lately?"

"No, thank goodness." Poppy flushed and lowered her voice to match Lyra's. "Sorry. Ms. Filmore makes me so nervous, and she's mean to Earl."

"I understand, but let's keep the fact that she's not your favorite customer between us, okay?"

Poppy nodded. "Okay, but I have to tell you that I and a lot of other people don't think it was very charitable that she didn't come to the wake."

"I'm sure a lot of people must have commented on it, but perhaps she was more upset than anyone gives her credit for."

"Upset? Ms. Filmore didn't like Rob."

"You don't think it was just for show?"

"No way. She was always bad-mouthing him to my mom."

Lyra glanced at Vanessa, who was watching them, and pulled Poppy though to the kitchen. "I didn't know your mom is friends with Arabelle."

"They go way back. That whole group does, although friends might be a little over-the-top these days, if you get my meaning."

Lyra smiled. "I do."

"The trouble with small towns is that you can't really stay away from someone for very long. You're bound to bump into them at the store, library, or the bar. And the diner," Poppy added as an afterthought.

"I've noticed that." Lyra let Poppy to go back to clear tables, and placed the empty tray on the counter. How on earth was she going to speak to Arabelle if the woman was hiding away? "Darn it," she muttered.

Leroy spun to face her. "What's up, boss?"

She hadn't meant for him to hear but saw no harm in

explaining herself. "I was hoping to catch up with Arabelle Filmore today."

"It's a bit early in the day for a round or two, isn't it?" he teased.

Lyra hedged. "I had something to ask her."

He glanced at the large clock above the cooker. "Arabelle feeds the ducks and other birds down at the village green about this time."

"I never knew that."

"It's hard to be interested in the people who don't conform to what we like to think of as acceptable behavior."

Lyra wasn't sure if he was censuring her or not. He'd returned to flipping burgers, and she clipped the new orders that spilled out of the machine on the rail beside him before heading out to the veranda. It was empty. Considering wiping tables for something to do, she suddenly decided on a new plan of action and went back inside. "Leroy, I'll be back in twenty minutes, okay?"

"We're all good here."

Smiling at Earl, who was diligently washing pots in the deep sink, Lyra headed back out to the veranda and down onto the gravel path where it split into two. Straight ahead led to the farmhouse, and the other direction turned right and went past the veranda, leading to an alley behind the other stores. This was the path she took and came out on the next road, which curved to the right. Now the park was on her left, and she crossed over the bridge to another gravel path, which led her toward the stream. Giant willows ran alongside the banks, and about halfway along the path was Arabelle.

A few yards from her, the woman must have heard her footsteps, and she turned toward Lyra.

"Hi, Ms. Filmore. I was out for a walk and saw you here. I haven't seen you for a while. How you are?"

Arabelle eyed her suspiciously. "This isn't your usual time of day to go walking. Aren't you too busy to be strolling around town?"

How did Arabelle know when she went for a walk? If she was watching Lyra from her house, that was a little troubling. "With all the baking I do, exercise is a must, and I'm never too busy to ask after a friend."

Her eyes narrowed. "Is that right? I wasn't aware that we were more than acquaintances."

"Surely after months of seeing you every morning, we're a little more than that? Plus, I've missed our little chats."

"Is business so bad you have to hunt customers down?" Arabelle scoffed.

The woman was impossible. "Business has never been better. Will you be coming back to the diner, or is it too sad to contemplate?"

"Why would I be sad? If you're thinking I'm missing Robert McKenna sparring with me...." She couldn't finish and turned back to the birds to throw bits of bread with a jerky motion.

Lyra didn't have to guess why. She'd seen the tears proving that Arabelle cared more than she wanted to admit. Lyra still wanted the fingerprint sample because Arabelle headed her list of suspects—despite now having second thoughts.

"If you like, I could drop off your favorite friand tomorrow. It's not like it would be any trouble since I have to go to the post office, which is near your house."

Arabelle tutted, then opened her handbag and took out a few dollars. She thrust them at Lyra. "That should be enough to keep your diner from going bust. Late morning would be best."

"Thank you. See you tomorrow." While she didn't run

back to the diner, it could hardly be called a leisurely walk, and she arrived slightly out of breath.

"Where did you go, and why do you look so smug?"

Lyra's hand shot to her throat as Mom came out from the pantry. "Good grief, you startled me."

Mom's eyebrows shot up. "Oh dear. That usually means a guilty conscience."

"What? No, it doesn't. I had an errand to run, but the cookbook's weighing on my mind, so I hurried back."

Mom raised her eyebrows again, but let it be. They'd developed an understanding about giving each other space, and Lyra's previous reservations over living together after so long proved to be unwarranted.

One day when Maggie and Dan moved on, and she hoped it wasn't for some time, Lyra wondered if those two would move in together. The way they acted around each other, it did seem logical.

Maggie was waiting on the last few recipes for the new cookbook, so Lyra hadn't lied about that, and she got out her laptop. Making a start on choosing which ones to include would be a good distraction.

"If you were looking for Maggie, she's down at the garage with Dan," Mom said as she began making the meatloaf that was one of the standard meals on the diner menu.

"I know. She's helping him understand the bookwork side of things."

"Do you think it should take all day and most evenings?"

Mom's wide-eyed innocence didn't convince Lyra for one second. "I hope you'll let them figure out their relationship for themselves."

"I haven't said anything to them." Mom tipped chopped herbs into the large mixer and added mince, sausage meat, and breadcrumbs. "Not really."

Lyra laughed. "They've known each other so long; it must feel awkward to transition from friends to something more."

"Huh. Don't you think transitioning is a fancy way of wasting time by not dealing with it head on?" Mom measured out stock, threw in eggs and garlic, then seasoning.

"I guess neither of them want to rush into anything or be gossip for the town."

"It constantly amuses me when a couple can't see that others know exactly what's going on." Chopping an onion, Mom sniffed. "Hiding how you feel never works, and like I say, usually there is no surprise when it comes to light."

"I guess they're a little wary to move from what they know to something new."

"Wary is fine. Taking too long is silly. You only have to see the people in Fairview who mucked things up by not taking a chance."

Now Mom had her undivided attention. "Who exactly are you talking about?"

Mom wiped her hands on her apron and came closer. "Rob and Arabelle of course."

Lyra gaped. Convinced until then that all this talk was really about her and Kaden, it took a moment to grasp what Mom said. "Do you mean they were in love?"

Mom nodded. "Deeply. There was a large group that hung out together since school, and when Rob's wife died, Arabelle stepped up to cook and clean for him. He was a mess and virtually shut down apart from his work. Hand on heart, I can say that there was no hanky panky. This was a friend helping a friend."

"But that changed?"

"It took a couple of years before they were seen out and about together. Arabelle was also cooking for him, and then began to eat her meals at his house. Sadly, some people were jealous, and the gossip got out of hand. Neither of them expected or could deal with that."

"So, they stopped seeing each other because of what other people were saying? That's terrible."

"It wasn't quite as simple as that. One weekend, on a rare visit, Rob had Phillip to stay and Arabelle came to make dinner. The boy must have seen how it was between them and threw a tantrum and wouldn't quit. The story goes that Rob asked Arabelle to leave so he could calm the boy down. That was the last time Phillip came to Fairview, and Rob blamed himself. He couldn't carry on a relationship in case Phillip changed his mind. That part Rob reluctantly admitted to your father and me."

"Meanwhile Arabelle was heartbroken."

Patricia nodded. "Poor Arabelle. She never married, and I believe it was in part because she had always loved Rob. Having waited all that time for him, and just when it seemed he might see her as something other than a housekeeper, he shut her out and kept out of her way. After a few years, they began the sniping you talked about. Martha also told me that it's a ritual that happens every morning and is one of the reasons Arabelle doesn't sit with the knitting ladies."

"One of the reasons?"

"Just between us, Martha said that Arabelle and Vanessa had a couple of dust-ups. Naturally they were over Rob, but it was also how Vanessa treated Poppy."

Maddie could imagine all of that playing out. Poppy and her mom certainly had a fractured relationship that revolved around Poppy's compliance. Lyra's heart was also sore for what might have been between Arabelle and Rob. Determined more than ever to speak to Arabelle, Lyra wanted to know if Phillip was the catalyst for her and Rob staying apart. Maybe his turning up this way had prompted a show-down, and Arabelle had lashed out?

But that would mean she would have had to know that Phillip was in town earlier. Besides, why would Arabelle hurt Rob and not Phillip? Because he basically jilted her?

And why would she hurt Leroy? That really didn't make sense.

29

Lyra carried a box of cakes through town and spied Carrie-Ann coming out of the food market. Noting that she carried a bag of apples, Lyra called out to her. "They're great at this time of year, aren't they?"

The woman swung around, almost smacking Lyra in the face with a bunch of flowers she held in her other hand. "What's that, dear?"

"I said the apples are delicious right now. I'm going to get some later and make pies."

"You make the best pies, no matter the filling. I'll use these for a sponge dessert I make, because I'd rather buy your pies."

"Thank you. Your dessert sounds nice too. Perhaps you could give me the recipe?"

"Really? I'll drop it by real soon, and then you can tell me what you think."

"Perfect. I'm always looking for something new to serve in the diner. Do you have a favorite pie?"

Carrie-Ann's eyes widened. "Why, I simply couldn't choose just one; I love them all."

Lyra laughed. "The knitting group's been busy. What are you working on?"

"At the moment we're knitting a bunch of things for the homeless and any newborns in the area."

"That's wonderful. Your knitting is the best I've ever seen."

"Well, I don't know if any of us can compare with Vanessa, but I like to think we all do a good job."

"You certainly do." Despite wanting to turn the conversation around, Lyra wasn't lying. She admired their skills and what the women did for the community. Carrie-Ann flushed with delight, and Lyra seized the moment. "Can I ask you a personal question?"

The woman giggled. "I'm an open book, dear."

This was turning out to be easier than Lyra imagined. "It's more to do with Vanessa. Poor Poppy is not happy, and I hear there's an issue with her mom on top of Rob's passing. I'd like to help her, so I wonder if you know what it's all about?"

Carrie-Ann moved her flowers to the arm holding the apples and tucked her arm through Lyra's, leading her away from the stores. "Vanessa wouldn't be happy with me saying anything about her private life, but if it's to help Poppy, then I'm almost obliged to do so, since I'm her godmother. Vanessa has that girl so wrapped up, Poppy can't say no to her mom for anything. Now, don't take this personally, but Vanessa never wanted her daughter to work for you. She thought you might lead her astray with your fancy lifestyle." She grimaced. "I mean the way it was."

"I see." Lyra shrugged. "Well, I can't change my past, but I'd like to assure her, and everyone else who may be thinking along those lines, that it wasn't as glamorous as it sounded. I worked very hard and had little time for partying."

Carrie-Ann smirked. "No boyfriends or scandal then?"

Lyra raised an eyebrow. "Everyone knows there was some scandal, but none I instigated. There were people working for me who were not honest, and I lost my restaurant because I trusted them."

Carrie-Ann patted her arm. "Oh dear, so the rumors are true about all your money being stolen."

"Maybe not all the money, nor all the rumors," Lyra teased.

"Rumors never are." Carrie-Ann winked. "And thank goodness you had enough to buy back your home and refurbish the diner. When the previous owner had it, the diner was simply somewhere for the knitting club to catch up for coffee instead of at one another's houses, which had become rather awkward with all the business over Rob. Since you came, that's all changed, and we're delighted to have a homely place that's clean. The Beagle Diner has become the hub of Fairview, and not just for us."

Lyra couldn't help the silly grin that stole over her. "That's so sweet of you to say. Fairview does feel like home again, and I missed it and the characters in it more ways than I can say, even if I don't feel that I knew people then the way I do now."

Carrie-Ann patted her arm. "You were so young when you left, and then you had all that fame. Goodness knows how you managed to make the transition back to small-town life."

"We all fall on tough times, and it's not always about money. From what I see around me every day, family and community are the most important things." Lyra gently steered the conversation back to where it needed to be. "Although Arabelle and Vanessa don't care for each other, do they?"

"Now that is a tricky situation. Fairview's not such a big place, and we all grew up together. Those two were best friends until they had a massive argument. It was a long time ago, but they can't seem to get over it. I've tried to get them talking, but it's like a cat fight when they're even in the same room."

"I have noticed. What was the fight about?"

Carrie-Ann glanced about them. "Not what, dear. Who?"

They were at the park by now, and Lyra stopped in her tracks. "What do you mean?"

"They were in love with the same man."

Mom's account of things was confirmed, albeit without the mention of Phillip's issues with Arabelle. There was only one man who fit the bill. "Do you mean Rob?"

Carrie-Ann winked. "We all would have loved for Rob to look our way. Stubborn man that he is, Rob only had room in his heart for one woman, and she died. Vanessa and Arabelle made it into some kind of contest. Unfortunately, there could never be a winner. Vanessa had been married, and to all accounts happily, but Arabelle only ever had eyes for Rob. It would have been fair for them to end up as a couple."

"That's so sad."

"Very sad indeed, and a little tragic to watch unfold. There's no point in the feud anymore, yet I can't see anything changing. Rob may have been stubborn, but those two do stubborn better than anyone I know. Now I should get on before my flowers wilt."

"Sorry to have kept you so long. Your next coffee is on me." This was a great excuse to get another set of prints. She had no reason to suspect Carrie-Ann, but the way she loved to tease Vanessa spoke of a slight wrinkle in her sweet persona. Lyra had seen the other side of people who exhibited the same characteristics, and it hadn't been pretty.

"How lovely. See you tomorrow. Bye, Cinnamon."

The beagle lifted her paw, and Carrie-Ann left with a chuckle. Lyra watched her turn into the street to the side of the park. Not only did Carrie-Ann live on that street, but two doors down was Arabelle's place. Both backed onto the park and then the stream. Lyra stopped at the end of the street to crouch and give Cinnamon a scratch.

"That was interesting, wasn't it?"

The beagle tilted her head.

"I have no idea if any of this latest information will help solve the crime, but if we're careful, we just might mend some fences."

Cinnamon woofed gently and licked her hand.

"Okay. Shall we walk through the park and try our luck with Arabelle?"

Mention of the *w* word as well as the *p* one had Cinnamon dancing on her back legs.

"Silly question. Let's go."

They wandered down the path so Lyra could look over the back of Arabelle's house, and found that there was a gate into the park just as there was at Carrie-Ann's house. A movement in one of the windows in Arabelle's house caught her eye.

"Aha! We better not go up the garden from here in case that's another of her pet peeves. Better to use the front door."

"Woof!"

"Plus, we might get a glimpse of any herb gardens on the way. I hope I can remember which ones we need to look out for."

30

The small section was immaculately kept with a box hedge along the walk trimmed into submission. Roses lined the path up to the house, each bloom perfection, and every plant a different shade of pink. There were no herb gardens in sight, front or back, unlike the other houses in the street. Which didn't mean that there were none down the sides or in the kitchen.

Lyra knocked and looked down at Cinnamon. "You might have to wait out here, okay?"

The beagle thumped her tail as Arabelle pulled back a curtain and peered through the glass panel of her front door. While she didn't exactly look delighted by Lyra being on her doorstep, she unlocked, then open the door.

"I suppose you want to come in. You and that silly mutt." Arabelle headed down a narrow hall and disappeared into the second room on the right.

Lyra and Cinnamon followed, both pleased by the invitation, as the beagle's tail smacking against the wall indicated. They entered a compact kitchen and combined dining room, where sun streamed in from the windows overlooking the tidy backyard they passed in the park. The decor appeared to be original, but was beautifully maintained, and the dining furniture could be considered art deco enough to be back in fashion.

Arabelle studied her curiously. "Tea?"

"That would be lovely."

"Hmmmph." Arabelle crossed to the range and heated water.

"Ms. Filmore, may I ask you a question?"

"If I say no, will you go away?"

Lyra gaped. There was no right way to answer that, because she didn't want to leave without some answers.

"I didn't think so. Take a seat." Then Arabelle did an amazing thing: she placed a bowl of water on the floor. "Don't make a mess," she warned.

Cinnamon dutifully took a drink, then sat at attention as Lyra put the box of friands on the table. Arabelle added two plates and knives as well as napkins, a small jug of milk, and a sugar bowl. She made the tea methodically, heating the pot first before adding tea leaves, then stirring it several times. When she brought it to the table, the pot wore a crocheted cover. Finally, she sliced a lemon and added that dish to the table before sitting opposite Lyra. Opening the box, she offered it to Lyra. "Help yourself."

Lyra waved away the offer. "They're for you."

"I won't eat more than one, and that's all I paid for. Unless you don't care for your own baking."

"Mostly I bake what I love. I think it makes a difference to the flavor." Lyra blushed at the admission and plucked out a friand.

"And the rest of the food you serve?"

"There's a certain expectation of food found in a diner, so Leroy cooks most of that, and between us we make what others tell me they love. Or what sells best, which I think is the same thing."

Arabelle nodded. "One can only assume that your celebrity business came about because you could actually cook."

This was a big admission, and Lyra smiled. "Every recipe I use, on my shows, in my books, or at the diner are tried many times before I decide if they're good enough."

"I'm pleased to hear that it's not some random selection. I too believe in doing your homework to get the best results. I also believe in not mincing words. Since I assume this is not exactly a social call, and that the friands were your way of getting to speak to me, I'd appreciate you telling me why you're here."

Lyra coughed on a few crumbs and was thankful for the napkin to hide behind while she got it under control.

"Drink some tea," Arabelle ordered.

Sure enough, a sip cleared the offending morsel, and Lyra dabbed her mouth and eyes. "Sorry about that."

Arabelle simply sat back and crossed her arms.

Lyra had the sudden feeling that she had better talk fast before Arabelle decided she wasn't interested in finding out Lyra's reasons for coming today and booted her out. "Here's the thing. I know that you're upset over Rob's death despite the animosity the two of you had."

"I won't deny that it affected me." Arabelle's eyes narrowed. "Just as everybody is affected when someone is murdered in a small town."

"At one stage you had been more than friends—"

"You can stop right there, missy. I am entitled to a private life, and what happened between Rob and me will stay that way."

"I understand the desire for privacy and wanting to keep a little something of yourself away from prying eyes. But as you said, this was murder. Don't you want Rob's killer to be found?"

Arabelle's teacup rattled in the saucer. "You think you know who it is?"

"I have my suspicions."

"Tell me."

"I can't. Not until I know for sure."

"I heard how you found a murderer a few months back." Arabelle leaned forward. "If that's true, how did you do it?"

"I weeded out everyone else. One at a time."

"So that's why you're here. I'm a suspect."

Lyra shrugged. "The truth is, we all are. Your relationship with Rob is a factor, but not the only one, because having a motive doesn't prove anything."

Arabelle steepled her fingers. "Whatever they killed him for, it wasn't because of me. What we had was long over."

Lyra nodded sadly. "He loved his wife very much, and I guess he was riddled with guilt when he decided that wanting you cost him his son."

Arabelle actually blushed. "The truth is that he did want me. We talked about it for months and how we would break it to Phillip. Rob was torn up inside over what he saw as his in-law's betrayal. They forced him to give up the boy, then made out that Rob wasn't sad about Dahlia's passing. That he'd moved on and didn't have room in his life for a child. Rob wanted to set the record straight. I tried to explain that children couldn't see through our eyes, that it was all about interpretation, and he needed to be patient when dealing with a child. If only I'd known that the sweet boy had been transformed into a spoilt and petulant child who didn't want his life upset by change. You see, he'd been indoctrinated by his grandparents to believe Rob was not only a cheat, but a liar. Rob's heart broke to hear these very words from his son, and he got angry. All that did was cement his preconceived ideas."

The picture of why Phillip was so angry was much clearer now. As was the reason that Arabelle and Phillip sparred so much. There was a saying that hate was the opposite of love, but it seemed that neither had truly hated the other. "It must have been incredibly hard when Phillip wouldn't accept you."

"More than anyone can imagine, but that was nothing compared to Rob's take on it. When Phillip refused to come back to visit, Rob decided he would bide his time and do so alone. He couldn't look me in the eyes or talk to me for years. In the end, I moved on."

Lyra sighed. "Only you didn't."

"What do you mean?"

"I saw you the night of the wake. You were across the stream, and terribly upset."

"That was you standing there?" Arabelle shrugged. "It was too far for me to be sure."

"You should have joined us."

"To what purpose? I'd said goodbye to Rob years ago. Standing around talking about him wouldn't bring him back. At least now he won't feel the guilt he carried every day."

Lyra wanted to reach out, but Arabelle wasn't the kind of woman who welcomed physical contact no matter how well-meaning. "I'm sure some of that was for you."

She shrugged again. "Maybe."

"I have to ask; did you go near the diner that night?"

"You mean, did I hit Leroy? What would be my motive?"

"Anger, resentment, sadness?"

"That's not how I deal with my emotions. Besides, I didn't have a gripe with Leroy."

Lyra nodded. Arabelle would have to be a sprinter to have attacked Leroy and gotten back to the stream. Besides Arabelle's way of dealing with things was to ensure she saw

Rob every day. Even if it wasn't exactly a satisfying encounter. Rob also could have changed the times he came into the diner. In a way, it was sweet, but there was still the catalyst for their unrequited love. "What about Phillip?"

"He was a child. Willful and distrustful. Unfortunately, he never grew out of that, and added a dose of vengefulness. His grandparents should take responsibility for that—I'm sure they won't. They blamed Rob for bringing their beloved daughter back to what they termed a hick town. They'd always wanted to be better than the rest of us and made a point of moving away. But Dahlia had made up her mind about Rob and went against their wishes. Using Phillip, the way his grandparents did, merely showcased their bitterness."

"So, Phillip's not to blame for his relationship with Rob?"

"Not initially. However, he is an adult and could have sought the truth and made amends. All he had to do was ask around Fairview."

"Maybe he tried. Did you speak to him?"

"Why would I? That would be like waving a red flag. I only wish I'd known the depth of his feelings before he arrived that day as a child. I would have done things very differently and somehow forced Rob to be more patient. There might have been a better outcome." Arabelle looked away. "Rob might still be alive."

"I don't think so," Lyra said gently.

They stared at each other for several seconds.

"You're probably right. And far more perceptive than I gave you credit for."

"Will you help me flush out the killer?"

Arabelle sipped her tea for a second or two. "I'll think about it."

"Thank you." Lyra finished her tea and cake, then stood. "I

have a bad feeling that whoever is causing trouble isn't done yet."

"Since they don't have what they want, I agree." Arabelle walked her to the front door.

"What do you think they want?" Lyra asked.

Arabelle shrugged. "The usual motives are revenge and money."

Lyra nodded. "I'd say that fits here. Do you have an opinion who it is?"

"I'm a senior, minding my own business. What would I know?"

"A lot more than some who talk too much. I've seen the way you watch people."

Arabelle smirked. "That makes two of us then, doesn't it? Thanks for stopping by."

The door closed, and the shadow stayed for a second or two before retreating. Instead of her mind being eased, it was running rampant as she went over every person who could possibly want to hurt Rob. Other than Phillip, who seemed more spiteful than murderous, the ones on her list didn't feel right.

She glanced at her watch and was surprised. Who would have thought that she and Arabelle would not only have sat down to tea but would have a civil conversation that would confirm everything Carrie-Ann and Mom told her? Sometimes gossip was born out of fact. Sometimes people weren't who you thought they were.

31

Lyra sat at the table in the farmhouse, having relayed the conversation. Now she waited for a response, which was a while in coming, as her mom digested things.

Finally, Patricia let out a sigh. "It was so long ago, it never occurred to me that they still had a thing."

"I didn't say that."

"No, but it makes some sense if you consider that hate is just a step away from love."

Lyra blinked a couple of times at hearing the same words she'd not long ago remembered. It was oddly reassuring to know that they still had similar thoughts on things. "So, they were needling each other because they were still carrying a torch?"

Patricia shrugged. "Stranger things happen."

A boom suddenly bent the air around them, and the windows shook. Lyra couldn't imagine that sound being an earthquake, so she ran out the front door and was just in time to see a ball of flame shoot up from the direction of the garage.

"I think there's a fire at Dan's place," she yelled, before

running down the steps and down the drive. When she saw for certain that it was the garage, a sickening roll of her stomach brought back the time she'd heard about Kaden's restaurant going up in flames. That had been because of her involvement with him. What if this was because Dan was her friend?

Mom followed, and Lyra heard her phoning the fire department. This was probably unnecessary since the station was around the corner at the top of the road and two doors down from the police station. They would surely have felt the bang and seen the flames from there. Just as she thought this, Lyra heard the siren, and seconds later a fire truck came around the corner.

Smoke billowed out of a car right in front of the building, and the door was alight. Outside, by the side of the road, Dan stood with a hose that made little difference to the inferno. Maggie was behind him, her hands covering her mouth.

"Are you okay?" Lyra asked, as she dragged Maggie across the road.

"It was so sudden. We'd been for a walk in the park with Cinnamon and were coming back here to do some paperwork. We weren't that far away when Vanessa's car exploded. Dan's supposed to be working on it tomorrow."

Lyra hugged her babbling friend just as the fire truck came to a halt and the volunteers jumped out. Once they had their equipment set up, they moved Dan away. It didn't take long until the flames were doused, but the air hung heavy with smoke still.

With a hangdog expression, Dan made his way to where they waited. "It will be a while before they can get inside, but it looks like only Vanessa's car and the door are damaged. Thank goodness I had everything locked up."

"Cars don't just explode," Lyra muttered.

He grimaced. "No, they don't."

"You think someone started this?" Mom asked.

Lyra looked around at the throng of people, which had grown until the shoulder on this side of the road was crowded. She kept her voice just loud enough for them to hear. "I'm almost certain. Clearly, someone isn't happy about Dan inheriting the garage."

She studied the faces and listened to what those closest were saying. It was hard to gauge whether they were all as horrified as she was, or merely curious. Did they understand that one or more among them could have killed Dan? Was that their intention, or was it simply to frighten him?

The fact that Maggie could have been hurt as well was even harder to accept. Lyra was not only angry, she was more determined than ever to find the culprit with or without Arabelle's help.

"Dan, could you come with me?" Walker nodded to Lyra and Mom before taking Dan several feet down the road.

"Wait here, Mom." Lyra followed the men.

Walker frowned and turned his back to her. "Did you see anything before the explosion, Dan?"

"Nothing. Maggie and I had been for a walk in the park, and we'd just returned when the car blew up."

"Do you have insurance?"

"Yes. Maggie organized it a couple of days ago."

"That's convenient."

Dan reared back. "Are you implying I did this? To what purpose? The car isn't mine, and I've spent hours getting the place ready to reopen tomorrow. I have clients organized, so burning down my garage would be pointless," he raged.

Walker shrugged. "Depends on how much the insurance is for."

"I can assure you that it's not a ton of money. I made it for the same as Rob had. I figured if it was good enough for him, then it would be fine for me. It will replace the car and

237

maybe the work I've already done on the front of the building. That's all."

The sheriff relaxed a little. "It's nothing personal. I just had to ask."

Dan nodded grudgingly. "Are you adding this to the growing list of sabotage and murder? And when exactly do you intend to find out who killed Rob, attacked Leroy, and flooded Lyra's house? I bet you'll find that it's the same person who did this."

Walker stiffened. "I can assure you that we're doing our best."

"Is that good enough? Maybe you need outside help so I can live my life without fear of something else happening to me or the people I care about."

Lyra had never heard Dan so angry, and the sheriff didn't seem to appreciate this.

"I heard that you plan to move in above the garage soon. It would be best if you stayed with Lyra for a little longer."

"And leave the garage open for another attack? I don't think so."

"Fine, but you can't stay here tonight," Walker growled.

When Dan puffed out his chest, Lyra stepped between them. "Leave it, Dan. The sheriff only means that they don't know what else someone might have tampered with, and there could be a hot spot somewhere still."

Dan blinked a couple of times. "Oh. I guess you do have to check inside and make sure of that."

"That's right, we do. I'll come by Lyra's tomorrow and explain the findings, if that's okay."

Dan shrugged. "Fine. I guess there's no point in staying, if I can't go inside."

"You're free to go. Could I have your keys, so we don't have to smash our way in?"

Dan pulled them from his pocket and handed them over.

Shoulders slumped, he walked slowly back up the road. Maggie ran behind him and put a hand on his arm.

"Thanks for calming him down," Walker said.

"He's naturally upset about this attack on the garage. He only has the place because Rob died, and he was so fond of the man that he wants to make a success of it to repay the trust."

Walker nodded. "I do understand, but I have a job to do, and it doesn't entail giving people privileges because they're sad."

It took a moment to digest this. Walker was right. There was a process, and everyone had to abide by it—if the process worked. Finding the person responsible was taking too long, and this was as good a time as any to tell him about her conversation with Arabelle.

"You might think that my opinion isn't enough to take Arabelle from the list, but I don't think she could ever hurt Rob because she was still in love with him."

"So, you didn't get her fingerprints?"

"There was no opportunity, but I'll have the whole of the knitting group tomorrow. I just need to be there to do the collecting without letting anyone else know about it."

"I guess that's better than nothing. I took prints off the receipt and the book it came from, which haven't turned up anyone I didn't expect. No, I better get back to the scene and find out how the fire started."

She bade him a good night and hurried to where Mom waited with Leroy, Poppy, and Earl, and they walked back up the road together.

"I still can't believe that just happened," Patricia announced grimly.

"Was the car faulty?" Poppy asked.

"No one knows yet. The fire department have their ways,

and they're bound to figure it out. Hopefully, something will lead us to the person who started it."

Mom tutted. "You'd have to have some terrible beef with Dan to do something so downright mean. I don't understand what, when he's such a sweetie."

Lyra studied each face as they walked away, wondering the same thing.

32

Lyra would love one night of decent sleep, but again she'd tossed and turned, and stumbled into the diner kitchen with a slight headache. It didn't help matters that Leroy was in a grump when he showed up.

After heating the grill, Leroy picked up a pair of gloves and waved them in the air. "Poppy, you're always leaving these darned things around."

"Sorry, I heard the bell and raced out front to serve."

He placed them under the sink with a firmness they didn't deserve, but turned quickly to apologize. "Don't mind me. I don't suppose any of us had a good night after that explosion. I hate to think that more businesses will be targeted."

Lyra had lain awake thinking the same thing, and now, watching Leroy, it washed over her again. Suddenly, her hands stilled in the dough she kneaded. Those plastic gloves he was so annoyed about protected their hands from the cleaning products they used. A month or two ago, she bought a box just for Poppy, since her hands were so small. This size only came in purple.

Waiting until Leroy was working the grill and Poppy left with the latest order, Lyra went over to the sink and reached underneath. That piece of plastic she'd seen stuck on the small skillet looked exactly like these gloves. She checked every inch of them, but they were intact. The trash from after the wake would have been collected days ago, so there was no way of proving that Poppy's gloves were involved—that Poppy was involved!

The thought blew her mind. She was so slight; how would Poppy have the strength to knock out Leroy? Lyra felt a little sick trying to imagine the scene. Plus, when all was said and done, Poppy adored Leroy. The day she started work, he'd taken Poppy under his wing, and when time permitted, he patiently taught her the basics of cooking. He was almost a father figure. She took a steadying breath. Hadn't Rob been the same for Poppy?

"Leroy?"

"Hmmm?"

"Poppy's been so upset lately, but she never gets angry."

He laughed. "Well, I wouldn't say never. She was furious about the person who hit me. And even angrier when the sheriff didn't arrest McKenna over that book business. You should have seen her going on about it. A little kitten with tiger claws—that's how I see our Poppy."

"Yes, she is tiny." Tiny enough to get through Lyra's bathroom window. Angry enough to put that receipt into the book. As the only one working in the diner when the book was found, she had the opportunity to do so without anyone noticing. But was she strong enough or tall enough to whack Leroy on the back of the head?

Poppy came back to collect another order and drop off a panini to toast. Lyra followed her out, and when she'd delivered the meal, Lyra called her to the counter.

"I've got a few things to do today, so I need your help.

Would you mind writing out an advertisement we can put in the paper for another waitress?"

Her eyes widened. "You're hiring more staff?"

"I think it's a good idea. You're often swamped, and while Maggie is great, it's not why she works for me. Wouldn't you like an assistant?"

"An assistant?" It only took Poppy a second to mull over the idea before she grinned. "That sounds cool. What should I say in the advertisement?"

"Just what the person would be expected to do. Pretty much your job but in a more junior role. Think you can handle it?"

Poppy took the paper and then glanced at the customers. "I'll have to do it in between serving."

"Perfect. I'll take it across to the newspaper office as soon as you're done. Meanwhile I can carry on with my errands."

Lyra left her to it and, working next to Leroy, finished off a stack of pancakes. If someone had suggested Poppy was involved in all this deception at any stage but now, she would have defended her to the end. Only, the end was in sight, and the clues were sticking together so well, it seemed as though Lyra had been barking up the wrong tree all this time. A little white lie was nothing compared to everything else.

"Excuse me for a couple of minutes. I have to make a call."

Leroy nodded absently, and Lyra chewed her bottom lip. This wasn't going to end well, and there wasn't a thing she could do about it. The thought of someone she cared about being so devious and, let's be honest, deadly, made her sick to her stomach. Who else would have been next if she hadn't noticed those gloves?

Lyra took her phone out onto the veranda. No, even with no one else out here, it was too close to the diner for this conversation. About to head to the farmhouse, she had another idea. If she was right, there was a major detail that needed checking. Running down the lane with Cinnamon at her heels, she raced along the path to the stream, where she scanned all the gardens at the back of the houses as best she could.

And found exactly what she was looking for.

On her return, she went straight to the farmhouse and around the side to overlook the stream from the opposite side. A breeze pushed the branches to make a sighing sound, which fit perfectly with how she felt as she dialed the sheriff.

"Walker."

His abrupt answer caught her off guard, and she found it difficult to form words with the lump in her throat.

"Hello?"

She swallowed hard. "It's Lyra. You need to get to my house now."

"Are you okay? What's happened?"

His concern was touching. "I'm pretty sure I know who killed Rob, hit Leroy, and started the fire."

"I'm listening."

"You'll think I'm crazy. It's Poppy."

"Yeah, I do find that hard to accept."

She heard the grin in his voice and hardened hers. "Believe me, I understand your reluctance. Let me explain."

He paused for a second. "Where are you?"

"Behind the farmhouse. I don't want to be overheard."

"That's wise when you're accusing a member of your staff."

"And someone I thought was a friend."

The phone cut off, which was odd. Surely, he wanted to hear exactly how she'd reached this conclusion. Unless he didn't take her seriously.

"All right. Why don't you try to explain?"

Her heart jumped, and she swung around to find him a few feet away. "You shouldn't sneak up on a person that way."

"I was headed to the diner anyway, so I cut around the corner and came straight here. Wasn't that what you wanted?"

"Yes," she said tersely, still a little put out by the fright. "Please keep an open mind until I'm done."

He raised an eyebrow, and she could swear that his mouth twitched. Well, he'd be laughing on the other side of his face if she was right.

33

An hour later, Lyra and the sheriff walked into the kitchen via the veranda door. Unfortunately, everyone was there, so there was no way of doing this quietly. Walker stepped forward and blocked the exit from where Poppy emptied her tray on the counter by the dishwasher.

"Poppy Fife, I'm arresting you on suspicion of murder, attempted murder, and arson."

Unaware of their arrival, Poppy gasped as the sheriff continued to read her rights. "What are you talking about?"

Leroy hurried from the grill, his face full of thunder. "Have you gone mad?"

"I'm afraid not. Poppy's glove got stuck to the skillet she used to hit you on the head," Walker explained.

Leroy laughed. "No way. Look at the size of her. She'd have to jump or stand on something. I'm pretty sure I would have heard that kind of commotion."

"From your statement, I understand that you were facing away from the attacker and bent over the dishwasher, humming along to music," Walker reminded him.

"Well, yes, but... it's Poppy." Leroy turned to the girl, who was ghostly pale.

Lyra gulped. She couldn't stand the way everyone was looking at her to make this go away. It would be best to get it all out in the open and deal with the pain all at once. "Poppy is the only one who fits the gloves found at the crime scene. She has access to herbs from her mother's garden and knows a lot about them. She was missing at the party when Leroy was hurt and first on the scene after the rest of us when the car at the garage caught fire. She's also small enough to get through my bathroom window. Isn't that right, Poppy?"

The young woman blustered as she looked around her for support. "This is crazy. I don't hurt people, and I don't steal."

"No one mentioned stealing," Lyra said sadly.

Leroy groaned. "You wouldn't hurt me, would you, Poppy?"

Her mouth opened and shut, and Walker moved forward with his cuffs out.

Poppy rounded on Lyra, and she snarled, "Why did you have to interfere? It was an accident."

"Exactly which part of this was the accident? Hurting Leroy, framing Phillip McKenna, or killing his father? Maybe you mean blowing up your mother's car or framing Dan? Tell us how you *accidently* stole from the diner, right underneath our noses."

Calling her out had the desired effect.

Poppy shrieked, showing her true colors at last. "What do you know about it? If Rob had married my mom, he would have taken care of us, and Mom could keep the Porsche."

Leroy groaned once more and slumped onto the chair Dan held for him.

Lyra glanced at the sheriff, who nodded his head for her to continue. "You seem to have overlooked that Rob wasn't in love with your mom. After working hard all his life, he had every right to do what he wanted with his possessions and who he wanted to live with."

"He was hated by his son, so it was silly that he still wanted to make amends." Poppy pouted childishly. "I'm the one who cared about him. I checked that he was eating right and made him meals. I listened to his endless stories and let him show me how engines worked. I could have been a daughter to him. Instead, he let a stranger move in, who watched me every time I visited."

The look she gave Dan was filled with hate.

"So, you broke into the house, flooded the bathroom, and left the note, as well as blew up your mom's car, but you were trying to scare off Dan, not me."

"Of course, it was Dan." Poppy smiled sweetly. "I love my job, and I don't want to go back to study except with you."

It all fell into place, and Lyra was filled with a sadness that warred with her anger. "And you wanted Dan to take the blame for poisoning Rob and hurting Leroy."

Walker pulled out his handcuffs and slapped them on Poppy's wrists just as Vanessa entered the room. By the sheer horror on her face, it appeared that she'd heard most, if not all, of her daughter's confession.

When Poppy struggled against the cuffs, Vanessa yelled, "That's enough. Don't say another word until I get you a lawyer."

The fight left her, and Poppy slumped against her mom. "I truly didn't mean to hurt Rob. I thought if he was a little sick from the herbs, you and I would take care of him, and he'd see that we could be a family. Then you wouldn't be so upset about me not earning enough money and having to sell your car, or ashamed that I didn't go back to school because I was hopeless at learning."

Vanessa looked so distraught; it was enough for Lyra to believe she hadn't had a hand in any of this. The insight into the why of Poppy's acts made it clear that she had orchestrated everything on her own. Nothing she said could excuse what she'd done.

"Messing around with Rob's medication was not only selfish and reckless, but incomprehensible when you say you cared about him. Likewise, Dan didn't deserve your attack on his good name, and Leroy showed you nothing but kindness. If you'd only asked, any one of us would have helped you sort out your finances." Lyra couldn't watch Poppy's realization at what being caught meant, and it wasn't in her nature to hurt the troubled girl further. As she was heading outside for some much-needed fresh air, betrayal swamped her. Sadly, this would cost Poppy her freedom for a long time, when she could have had a career.

Would she use the time wisely and reflect on her misdeeds and get well? It would be difficult to get over the fact that Rob lost his life because of her and that Leroy could also have died. Plus, she'd terrorized the whole town. Even if it were possible, that was a lot to make up for.

Sitting on the veranda with the sun setting, a sparkle of light hit the horizon. Opposite the farmhouse, the park rose, and a wide ribbon of different shades of green spread towards the sky. Lyra looked over the hedge to her left, where Rob should have been tinkering away in his garage.

The others came and went, saying nothing about managing the diner while she digested everything, simply making sure she was okay. They had to be struggling too, and Leroy more so. She wanted to console them but was sapped of energy and welcomed a level of blankness.

It was quite a while later when Walker came out the door. After a heavy sigh, he took a seat beside her.

"Great view."

She nodded.

"This must hurt, but you have to know that you did the best you could for Poppy."

She was touched that he'd picked up on what troubled her. "If I had, I would have noticed that she was broke and how bad her fixation with Rob was. He was such a nice guy; I thought that she was simply responding to that because she had no father figure."

"A bit like you and Rob."

Lyra let that sink in. "I guess so. He made me feel good about everything. Even the little stuff."

"I liked him too."

She gave him a side-eye. "He didn't think you did."

"I disagree. We had a run in when the developers hit town, and he thought I was selling Fairview down the river. That's the trouble with being the sheriff in small towns, you can't please everyone. Besides, Rob was entitled to his opinion."

"It must be hard trying to please everyone," she acknowledged.

He laughed. "Let me tell you, that's never gonna happen, and I gave up on it a long time ago. But I was glad you swept in and bought the diner before they got ahold of it. Doing that helped others in the street stick to their guns and hold on a bit longer. Slowly but surely, things have turned around, and people are making money again. That's all down to you."

"You mean who I used to be."

"Lyra, you will always be the celebrity chef and TV star around Fairview, no matter how long you live here."

She shook her head. "Very few people comment on it anymore, which I don't mind at all."

"Hah. Maybe not to you, but the people of our town are still talking about their famous resident to each other and outsiders. Regardless of how you feel about it, you've put

Fairview on the map, which is something the town has needed and wanted for a very long time."

"I never thought of that. I suppose there are a lot of out-of-towners these days who stop by for more than an hour or two."

"Exactly. Which means there's income coming in that there normally wouldn't be. People might not thank you for that, but it's the truth and makes a huge difference to the town's survival. You should be proud."

She shook her head in wonder. "I love the idea of others benefiting in some way. Thanks for making me feel a little better."

Walker smiled warmly. "Glad I could. So, what next for Lyra St. Claire?"

"Wow, you move on fast."

"No point in letting this eat at you. If I did that, I'd high-tail it out of this town and to heck with disappointment."

That made her smile. "I have too much invested, so I can't do that. I guess I'll advertise for a new waitress and finish my book. That will be enough for now."

He raised an eyebrow. "And maybe stay away from any mysteries?"

"I'd like to make that promise, and as long as the town has no more steak secrets, it shouldn't be a problem."

He laughed. "Then I better have a word with Cinnamon and make sure she chooses her friends more wisely."

The beagle's ears twitched, and she lay at Lyra's feet with her paws over her face.

Lyra scratched her head. "What do you mean?"

"All that missing steak was in Rob's kitchen. Poppy confessed to pretty much all of the crimes. She had a key to the house as well as the diner. She thought that Phillip would mention it being there and I would pin the theft on Dan. Cinnamon's love of Poppy is mainly due to her being fed steak to keep her quiet while Poppy went about stealing things to sell from Rob's place."

Cinnamon crawled under the seat, whacking her head, and faced away.

Lyra chuckled. "That explains why she wouldn't eat her meals. She does seem ashamed by her actions."

"It's okay, Cinnamon." He grinned at Lyra. "We all make mistakes."

She wasn't sure if that comment was only about Cinnamon. "I suppose Phillip had no idea what was there, so he didn't miss the thefts."

"That's right. We found a few items in Poppy's room at Vanessa's house that Dan might be able to confirm are Rob's. The pantry was bursting with food, but of course there's no way we can prove any of it is yours."

Lyra peered under the chair. "Did you know about this, Cinnamon?"

The brown tail tucked tight underneath her, and the beagle hid her face again.

Walker grinned again. "I swear this dog understands every word we say."

"I've never doubted it. Do you have to get back to the station, or can you stay for coffee?"

"I do have to get back, and I'm sure your staff would like to talk to you. However, I'd love a takeaway coffee, and maybe one of those chewy chocolate chip cookies?"

Despite the terrible events, Lyra laughed. It really was the only way to deal with the situation that would indeed hurt them all for some time, and she was grateful that the sheriff wasn't belaboring the fact that she'd once more interfered.

There was one more matter to attend to. No matter that she wasn't fond of Phillip, he deserved an apology.

EPILOGUE

Sitting on the veranda after closing the next night, Lyra was surrounded by her team. The evening was warm, the sky sprinkled with stars.

Leroy sat at a table, despondently nursing a coffee. Lyra had pushed him to take the day off but asked him to stop by this evening along with the others. Touching on a couple of things last night, she'd chosen now to talk about the events of the last twenty-four hours without interruptions from customers, and because she felt they'd had time to digest all the information.

She stood in front of them, hoping for an open and honest discussion that might help towards the healing needed. "We can't push this under the carpet and pretend it never happened, and the only way we'll move forward is to talk about Poppy. What she did is unconscionable, but I believe she's unwell and probably has been for some time. She needs help."

"Help?" Maggie yelped. "After what she did?"

Dan put his hand on Maggie's shoulder and pulled her back onto the seat that ran around most of the veranda.

"Lyra's right. You heard what Poppy said. She thought she and her mom would get a better life if he was a little sick and they took care of him. Her ignorance killed Rob."

"What about selfishness?" Maggie said tersely.

Lyra nodded. "Yes, she was selfish, but didn't you say that you felt sorry for her because of Vanessa? Her road wasn't the easiest."

"So, whenever life gets tough, we should fix it by any means possible?"

"Not at all. I'm just saying we shouldn't throw stones."

"I don't understand any of this," Earl broke into sobs. "My friend isn't capable of killing a person, let alone Rob or Leroy. Poppy knew I had learning difficulties and she never put me down."

Patricia bundled him into her arms. "As Lyra says, the Poppy who did this isn't well. She got tangled up and lost sight of the harm she was inflicting."

Just then a car pulled up the drive of the farmhouse.

"What now?" Lyra muttered.

A door slammed and footsteps crunched on the gravel before Kaden burst through the opening in the hedge.

How did he know she needed him here?

She ran down the steps to meet him, and he scooped her up.

His heart thumped against hers. "Maggie called me. I came as fast as I could. You have to stop playing detective."

"I will when people behave themselves," she muttered into his neck.

He put her down and took her hand. They walked slowly back to the group, who gathered around them. Except now there was one more.

For a change, Sheriff Walker was out of uniform. He wore jeans and a shirt, which made him look less cold. Although the hard stare at Kaden was definitely chilly.

"I saw the light on and thought I better check on the diner. I came up through the alley."

Lyra dropped Kaden's hand. "Sorry. I should have told you we were having a meeting to talk about... everything."

Suddenly, Walker grabbed her arm and pushed her behind him as a shadow loomed at the hedge behind Kaden who, frowned and was about to say something. That's when they noticed Walker's hand searching his hip and come back empty.

"Who's there?" Walker shouted.

The shadow came into the light. "Phillip McKenna."

"What do you want?" Walker asked, his voice icy.

"A minute of your time, Lyra. If you don't mind?"

Surprised, at not only his request but the pleading tone, she nodded at Walker. "Let him up."

Everyone moved back on the veranda, and Phillip climbed the few steps to stand awkwardly in front of them. "I owe you all an apology. Sheriff Walker explained the story—in more detail. I can honestly say that I had no idea about any of it. Which doesn't make my attitude right. I'd like to apologize for being so unreasonable. We had nothing in common, but Dad wrote me all about the people in Fairview."

Lyra, like the rest of them, waited while he rubbed a hand over his face and took a deep breath.

"I have boxes of letters. All they did was make me angry and jealous, so I stopped reading them. I don't know why I brought them with me, but last night I decided to go through them. The way he talked about everyone was how I wanted someone to feel about me. And the way you all spoke about him since I've been here, well, there's too much evidence to deny that he was a good man, and this is a great place to live." His voice shook, and Phillip took another moment to compose himself.

"My grandparents gave me everything I asked for. I just

didn't understand that the one thing that mattered I could have had if I hadn't listened to what they said about Dad. After I'd read the letters, which I intended to burn as... I don't know, some kind of cleansing, I went looking for evidence of his love. I found cards he bought but never sent, along with more letters. He said he was proud that I had my own business and that he hoped fixing computers brought me joy the way fixing cars did for him. I guess we had more in common than I wanted to believe. Which means that what you've been through could have been avoided if I had been a better son."

Mom patted his arm. "You aren't to blame, dear. Circumstances beyond your control swept in and made this perfect storm."

"Thank you, ma'am, but I'd still like your forgiveness. Especially you, Dan. You made his last months happy, and I can be grateful at least for that. He was right to leave you the garage. I haven't got a clue about machines of any description except computers. Dad knew that." He stuck his hand out.

After a brief hesitation, Dan took it with both of his. "I never asked or expected anything from your dad except friendship. He was a great mechanic and an even better friend."

"I would have liked his friendship. When I saw him working at the garage, his passion and enjoyment for his work came through. I wish I'd given him a chance to teach me how to feel that way."

Lyra chewed this over as Cinnamon sniffed at Phillip, who crouched and scratched the beagle's head. She licked his hand. It was both strange and heartwarming after his coolness toward her all this time. The good-natured pooch obviously harbored no hard feelings. "Maybe he's given you a chance instead."

Phillip squinted up into the light of the veranda. "What do you mean?"

"Well, you have a house in Fairview." She nodded over the hedge. "Maybe you could hang around a bit longer and take time to meet the people who shared his life. It might give you more of an idea of the man he was and give you closure."

His eyes widened. "You want me to stay after all I've said and done?"

"I'm not saying it will be rainbows and butterflies, but why not?" Lyra winked. "At least you know where to find a great steak."

"Just one?" he asked deadpan.

There was silence for a second before Maggie snorted. That led to a chuckle from Dan and Kaden, then the rest of them laughed until some shed a few tears.

Lyra gazed around at these people who meant so much to her. She included the often-grumpy sheriff, who had lately shown a different side she rather liked, and the change-of-heart stranger who had grown up a confused and angry boy. He'd changed in the shortest of times, and Lyra knew Rob would be proud of him.

Kaden shared her look of happiness, and that made things perfect, along with Cinnamon who danced around them, clearly done with her battle of steak overload. Things were definitely looking up, and hopefully there would be a little peace in Fairview.

That would be nice.

Thanks so much for reading Beagles Love Steak Secrets, the second book in the Beagle Diner Mysteries series. I hope you enjoyed it.

If you did…

1 Help other people find this book by leaving a review.

2 Sign up for my new release e-mail, so you can find out about the next book as soon as it's available and pick up a bonus epilogue. If you've previously joined my newsletter, don't worry, you'll be able to get it very soon for free.

3 Come like my Facebook page.

4 Visit my website caphipps.com to view all my books.

5 Keep reading for an excerpt from Book 3 Beagles Love Muffin But Murder.

BEAGLES LOVE MUFFIN BUT MURDER

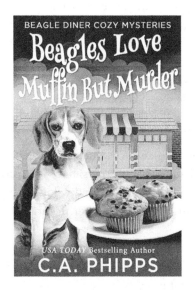

Cinnamon raced along the stream and disappeared into the undergrowth of a copse of trees. Excited barks meant she'd located a squirrel or other equally fascinating animal. What the beagle wanted was for the creature to run so she could give chase and Lyra waited for whatever it was to be flushed out.

Whatever was in there wasn't in any hurry and Lyra needed to get back to the diner. "Cinnamon! Let it be. Come on, girl," She called loudly to be heard above the barking, but the beagle continued.

Usually obedient, Lyra had no choice but to go see what was giving her pooch so much grief. A flattened patch of grass gave way to small broken branches and a patch of sun that managed to get through the overhead branches shone on something. It must be a piece of metal and if it was sharp it could injure an animal.

Crouching, Lyra duckwalked closer. The metal turned out to be the rim of sunglasses which lay on the ground next to a man. He stared at her with a look of surprise.

What was he doing laying in here like that? "Hello. Sir? Are you okay?"

He didn't so much as blink. The sinking in her stomach could not be denied. She pushed aside the rest of the lower branches to see that he was bent in a funny angle—and a knife stuck out from his chest.

Lyra recoiled, then forced herself to feel for a pulse. He skin was cool and there was no sign of life. Scrambling back out of the bush she looked around wildly. She had no phone and needed to contact the Sheriff. Arabelle's' place was closest.

"Cin. Wait here."

The beagle crept toward the man and lay down with her head on her front paws.

"Good girl. I'll be as fast as I can."

Thank goodness for sensible shoes. Lyra pumped her arms and legs and made it to Arabelle's gate in a couple of minutes. She slammed through it and ran up the path to pound on the back door.

It swung open. "What is all this ruckus for?" Arabelle demanded.

"I need the sheriff," Lyra gasped.

The man in question peered around Arabelle.

"Thank goodness you're here. A man's been murdered in the park."

He slapped his hat on his head. "Let's not jump to conclusions."

"I'd say no pulse and a knife in the chest makes things kind of obvious."

Get Beagles Love Muffin But Murder today!

RECIPES

These recipes are ones I use all the time and have come down the generations from my mum, grandmother, and some I have adapted from other recipes. Also, I now have my husband's grandmother's recipe book. Exciting! I'll be bringing some of them to life very soon.

Just a wee reminder, that I am a New Zealander. Occasionally I may have missed converting into ounces and pounds for my American readers.

My apologies for that, and please let me know—if you do try them—how they turn out.

Cheryl x

COTTAGE PIE

Ingredients

500g / 1.1lbs ground beef (use venison for a lean alternative)

Tin of tomatoes or 6 medium fresh (scald with hot water and remove skin)

2 tsp cooking oil

2 tsp garlic

3 tsp mixed herb

1 tbsp Worcestershire sauce

1 finely chopped brown onion

1 finely chopped carrot (1 cup of mixed veggies is a quick alternative)

8 medium potatoes

1 dstspn butter

1 cup milk

1 cup grated cheese

Instructions

In a frypan, brown beef in oil.

Add onions and cook until soft then add garlic.

After a couple of minutes add the herbs, Worcestershire sauce, and season with salt and pepper.

Cook down until the mixture has thickened.

Meanwhile peel and quarter the potatoes and boil in salted water.

When soft, mash with butter, adding enough milk to make spreadable.

Put the meat mixture in an oven-proof dish and spread potato on top.

Sprinkle with cheese and grill until brown.

Serve with broccoli florets or beans.

Tips: This is the perfect recipe to use any leftover vegetables or soft tomatoes and you could add some chili to spice it up. ;-)

ALSO BY C. A. PHIPPS

Beagle Diner Cozy Mysteries

Beagles Love Cupcake Crimes

Beagles Love Steak Secrets

Beagles Love Muffin But Murder

Beagles Love Layer Cake Lies

The Maple Lane Cozy Mysteries

Sugar and Sliced - Maple Lane Prequel

Apple Pie and Arsenic

Bagels and Blackmail

Cookies and Chaos

Doughnuts and Disaster

Eclairs and Extortion

Fudge and Frenemies

Gingerbread and Gunshots

Honey Cake and Homicide - preorder now!

Midlife Potions - Paranormal Cozy Mysteries

Witchy Awakening

Witchy Hot Spells

Witchy Flash Back

Witchy Bad Blood - preorder now!

The Cozy Café Mysteries

Sweet Saboteur

Candy Corruption

Mocha Mayhem

Berry Betrayal

Deadly Desserts

Please note: Most are also available in paperback and some in audio.

Remember to join Cheryl's Cozy Mystery newsletter.
There's a free recipe book waiting for you. ;-)
Cheryl also writes romance as Cheryl Phipps.

ABOUT THE AUTHOR

'Life is a mystery. Let's follow the clues together.'

C. A. Phipps is a USA Today best-selling author from beautiful New Zealand. Cheryl is an empty-nester living in a quiet suburb with her wonderful husband, 'himself'. With an extended family to keep her busy when she's not writing, there is just enough space for a crazy mixed breed dog who stole her heart! She enjoys family times, baking, and her quest for the perfect latte.

Check out her website http://caphipps.com

Made in United States
Orlando, FL
03 September 2024

51034498R00168